KW-223-549

'Very exciting… most beautifully written… its words as carefully chosen as the words of a poem" – A. S. Byatt, Radio 3

"The shape-shifting nature of its plot, and a precision of language which serves to enhance its mystery, are the chief pleasures of *Flying to Nowhere*" – Adam-Mars Jones, *Sunday Times*

"A masterly performance… a significant fictional debut"
– *Glasgow Herald*

The Adventures of Speedfall

"A dazzling new farce—a sort of *Yes, Principal* version of the academic corridors of power…" – Gillian Greenwood, *The Literary Review*

"At last the real thing" – Nicholas Best, *Financial Times*

"This is an elegantly written and frequent hilarious collection"
– *Sunday Times*

"Donnish humour at its most urbane, ingenious and eccentric"
– John Mellors, *The Spectator*

Tell It Me Again

"An abiding pleasure" – *Evening Standard*

The Burning Boys

"A striking and clever short novel about a boy growing up, set in the Forties, but with insights that are not dated" – Philip Howard, Novel of the Week, *Observer*

"Superb… a novel of special quality" – *Evening Standard*

"Here is a short book whose size is not tailored with an eye to fashion but with a sure sense of what is artistically right. Wherever you cut it, the aces are high, the story rich" – Candia McWilliam, *Guardian*

Look Twice

"Sheer fun… it is indeed enormously and intelligently entertaining; its pace and flair is such that it would make a breathtaking, if prohibitively expensive, film" – Nick Hornby, *Sunday Times*

"It's funny, it's clever and it is great great fun" – *Evening Standard*

"Tantalising and amusing" – *Sunday Telegraph*

The Worm and the Star

"*The Worm and the Star* is a lesson in structure to novelists, a lesson in clarity to poets, and, to readers, a deeply civilised and civilising gift" – Glyn Maxwell, *Guardian*

A Skin Diary

"Superb" – *Times Literary Supplement*

"In part the novel is about language itself and sees Fuller, who has written more than 30 books of poetry and prose, in full flight" – Russell Celyn Jones, *Times*

"Rich and marvellous writing indeed" – James Jauncey, *The Scotsman*

"Fuller's imagistic flair and delight in language conjure an elemental magic" – Jason Thompson, *Harpers & Queen*

The Memoirs of Laetitia Horsepole

"This is an extraordinarily good novel. Deftly clever and full of fun. [It] tells us more about being female and smart in Georgian England than a whole slew of social history books ever could" – Kathryn Hughes, *Daily Telegraph*

"Fuller combines intelligence and ravishing lyricism with a gorgeous gift for storytelling… Fuller is something special. Those who want to give their reading clubs something pleasurable to tackle should put their hands up for Laetitia. She won't let them down" – *Literary Review*

Flawed Angel

"*Flawed Angel* is a philosophical tale in the style of *Rasselas*, and Fuller devises, with great ingenuity, a society that has tried to provide civilised solutions to eternal problems" – A. S. Byatt, *Guardian*

"A repertory of wonders… this fairy tale will surely outlive him" – *The Times*

"Sumptuously written… a curiously beautiful and life-affirming story" – *Telegraph*

"A delicious treat" – *Guardian*

"A novel as intellectually provocative as it is emotionally beguiling" – Lucy Powell, *Observer*

THE CLOCK IN THE FOREST

THE CLOCK IN THE FOREST

JOHN FULLER

Shoestring Press

Printed by imprintdigital
Upton Pyne, Exeter
www.digital.imprint.co.uk

Typesetting and cover design by narrator
www.narrator.me.uk
info@narrator.me.uk
033 022 300 39

Published by Shoestring Press
19 Devonshire Avenue, Beeston, Nottingham, NG9 1BS
(0115) 925 1827
www.shoestringpress.co.uk

First published 2019
© Copyright: John Fuller
© Cover image, Apollo and Daphne by Gian Lorenzo Bernini.
Culture, baroque. (ID 91498443) © Polina Sister |
Dreamstime.com

The moral right of the author has been asserted.

ISBN 978-1-912524-06-8

To my grandsons, with love.

CONTENTS

1. Forgetfulness

There are side streets in the busy avenues of our lives. And yes, we are often so busy that we forget that we have ever actually been into them. The roar of destination deafens us.

Some strange chance took me, with half an hour to kill, into Cecil Court, that little passageway of bookshops off the Charing Cross Road, where the traffic is momentarily muffled and the boxes of bargains slow the pace. I was due at the Heinz Archive of the National Portrait Gallery, to look for images of the Hampshire neighbours of Lydia Arnold after her amazing marriage to the 7th Earl of Cavan in 1814. And I found something quite different, which knocked me sideways.

Somebody once wrote that forgetfulness protects us against boredom. That's to say, life is too boring to be tolerable if we are aware of all that has happened to us. Which is why we conveniently forget half of it. Or is it supposed to be three-quarters of it? Or even more? I forget.

And there is said to be an art of forgetting; of knowing which quarter of it is worth remembering.

I'm not so sure that forgetting doesn't better protect us against fatalism. It helps us to disconnect the depressing chain of cause and effect, to escape determinism, even sometimes to be quite surprised by our own lives. I thought my own life pretty secure. I was safely on track to think what I think, to feel what I feel and to produce what I produce.

Ah, Lydia Arnold. That is quite another story. This story is not at all about Lydia. Although I was half in love with this practically invisible centre of the bustle of Regency life that I was investigating, as I accumulated the lost fragments of her existence with a kind of attenuated frenzy. I wasn't sure what I could make of it all. I could pretend that it was research, and certainly I was eager to stick closely to the plain truth of her life and of the other lives touched by her, but the more I discovered, the more remote she seemed. She perfectly embodied an old theory of mine about the substitutions of fiction.

Since this theory applies pretty directly to what you are about to read, perhaps I should bother to explain it. But Lydia is only the hook. The theory isn't intended as a rebuke to our cruel forgetfulness or deficient sentiments, nor is it an attack on fiction (though such attacks have been made in all seriousness, and I suppose that they are respectable enough to need answering). Anyway, here's the thing.

Who do you know more about, your great-grandmother or the heroines of novels contemporary with her?

Yes, it's a simple question, and it puts us on the spot, doesn't it? In my own case, the question will weigh my own great-grandmother Amanda Hoyle against her fictional contemporaries Sue Bridehead, say, or Carinthia Kirby. You can work out your own examples for yourself. With whom do you feel more intimate, more involved?

You'll probably complain that your great-grandmother has no story, is not indeed herself a story in the sense that heroines are their own stories. You are unlikely to have known your great-grandmother at all. But that's my point. We have managed to substitute for our family history, and therefore to a great extent for history itself, this spurious fictional alternative. Our whole sense of the century before our own is alive and busy, not with the biological reality that ultimately gave birth to us and our own consciousness, but with elaborately detailed inventions which can't possibly have anything to do with it at all. We have filled our heads with these great imaginary substitutions, and should admit, if we are honest, that we truly believe in them.

It was the case, too, with this foray of mine into biographical research. I had begun to feel that however much I might discover about Lydia Arnold, I should never be able to know her as I know Emma Woodhouse or Di Vernon or Lucy Snowe. Them I believe in. To all intents and purposes they may be supposed to have some sort of existence. I have been told (and this is the significant thing) exactly what happened to them.

Suppose I were to hook down the WAT-WRI box-file in the Heinz Archive and find by chance an engraving of Emma Woodhouse? I would be shocked, of course, at the flagrant imposture. It would violate the secure sense of her as the most irritating but somehow faceless heroine of Jane Austen's that I possess somewhere in my innermost consciousness. She would be quite as unbelievable as Gwyneth Paltrow.

Conversely, I could never want to invent anything about Lydia Arnold. The slightest conjecture seemed to me immensely dangerous. I wanted only facts. I could hope for no more from Cecil Court than some prints (a country house in her neighbourhood perhaps, settled in its sculpted park like a toy on a sofa) or some old newspapers.

But what I did discover, as my fingers flicked over a rack of bargain CDs, was a disc of British music from a label unknown to me, and with a distinctly hideous cover, in abstract shapes of buff and lime-green vaguely suggestive of oak-leaves. Its title was *Five Post-War Romantics*, and I only turned over this unpromising collection to see if it had something by a woman composer in it, so that I might buy it for my daughter Sophie, who is an expert in that field. No women featured, but what it did contain (and I saw the name there with a full and mysterious sense that I had known beforehand that it would be there, known perhaps even before I had entered the shop) was the Arne Piano Concerto.

This is the corollary of forgetting: the chance remembering. The Arne Piano Concerto! Of course. It would have had to be there, as I immediately realized, in that hopeful little gathering of forgotten austerity rhapsodists. It was so utterly representative of

3

its period, when wartime partings and hardship had nudged the soul off once again on its dreamy explorations, and music was unafraid of passion and sentiment. It wasn't true, perhaps, that this was an absolutely forgotten handful, for Alan Rawsthorne was among them. I rather like Rawsthorne, as a matter of fact, who I think of as a kind of ferocious but melancholy English Hindemith, certainly not dreamy. Well, no doubt he was there as a bait, with a brief dance suite that I had never heard of, out of copyright probably, or otherwise cheaply obtainable.

The others were quite forgotten, Arne not least, and most of all (I realised with a strange emotion of regret, guilty recollection and overpowering curiosity) by me. It was I myself, I knew, as I stared at the listed concerto ('I: Andante malinconico 6.12; II Largo funèbre 5.20; III Scherzo giocoso 3.50; Moderato risoluto 6.23') who had forgotten him. If everybody else had forgotten him as well, that was their look-out. But I felt a lurch of neglected responsibility. He had passed from my life, and therefore from my mind, and I was convinced at that moment that my having forgotten him was the major cause of his utter neglect as a composer, and that my happening to pick up this disc was a significant personal rebuke, in some way fatefully intended, as these moments can so often seem to be, against all reason.

What laughable superstition! But in its most extreme form this kind of guilt can erupt in some surprising scenarios. I have woken from a dream and continued for some time, in full consciousness, to believe that I had once indeed committed the murder that in the dream I was trying to hide. This conviction was always quite precise, however vague the general circumstances, containing the memory of previous occasions when I also remembered that I was a murderer, together with circumstantial detail and the inescapable realization that it was now too late to return to a time of innocence. The likely faults that fed such an extreme symbol would have seemed pretty insignificant had they offered themselves to the sleeping mind tortured and gripped by them. But we are sometimes in that rare mood when we can look clearly at our misbehaviour and are often quite surprised that it has escaped punishment, or perhaps hasn't even been much noticed.

It must be laziness rather than cowardice that stops us being more attentive prosecutors in the perpetual sessions of our own lives. We have much to punish ourselves for, and when we do it we gain a kind of satisfaction. We reach into the margins of our consciousness for the assembled evidence.

Which was the place where I had driven Maurice Arne and his concerto. They had for decades inhabited an unvisited limbo in my mind, that place of lies, betrayals and impostures which religious tradition requires to be cleansed by confession. I, with no religion, knew very well that this limbo must always remain what it is, a place of accumulation and insistence, unchangeable, and without forgiveness. To live with it is simply to come to terms with what it is, and therefore with what we are ourselves.

Perhaps coming across *Five Post-War Romantics* was, therefore, like coming across an empty confessional box in a dusty church visited as a tourist, a ready reminder of what acts of contrition are no longer possible, the rich and responsible life of the past forever turning, as it does, into a mere aesthetic spectacle. Coming out into the summer drizzle with the CD in my briefcase (it always seems to drizzle in Cecil Court) I felt that I had both suffered a momentary arraignment in my private dock and also ticked off in my moral guide-book a place to be visited. The business, however, wasn't finished there. Some kind of door had been opened.

But it took something else to get me through the door. It took a coincidence of the kind that underlines the apparent purposes of fate in re-routing our thinking by reminding us of things that we may have conveniently forgotten. These things are mutually dependant. Would we even believe in coincidences if we remembered absolutely everything? We would have no random narrative to reconstruct. Everything we experienced would be of equal value, and it would occur again and again in different forms and circumstances until it was virtually meaningless. And we would automatically connect everything with everything else, and it would have no need to make sense. A coincidence could never be extraordinary.

But they are, of course. Like the one that occurred later in the summer, when the drizzles of July had yielded to the wild fruits of September, when holidays had been taken and the first duties of the autumn arrived. And the coincidence seemed designed to enforce a serious attention to this memory already evoked. It too was bound up with forgetfulness, or at least with things which I thought I had forgotten.

I had been invited once again to my favourite literary festival, the one at King's Lynn that seasonally alternates its attention between poetry and fiction. It is a small affair, run with a relaxed generosity and careful attention to detail by a local solicitor, Tony Ellis. The whole point of it is for the invited writers to reacquaint themselves with the faithful local audience, to quiz each other and report on their work in public, and generally to have a good time. The writers are met on Friday noon at the railway station with champagne and bagpipes, and in return for such treats are induced to appear at local schools and to be more or less continuously on call for the whole week-end.

Intimacy is the order of the day. Writers are billeted with members of the committee. There is no hiding, no escape from question-and-answer sessions, no off-duty moments or retreat from scrutiny. But there is plenty of food and drink, and good company.

Which is why, after my last reading and during the signing of copies, I greeted each request with something more than a formal smile, and with a readiness to continue talking about topics that had already come up during the session. Many of those who wanted my signature I knew already, even by name. I knew the sort of things they were interested in.

But at the end of the queue there was one woman, I guessed in her early sixties, with my volume in her hand open at the title page ready for my pen, whom I had never seen before and yet who had on her face the oddest expression of mixed timidity and knowingness. A committee-member (a woman of similar age, whom I did know) was at her elbow, saying brightly:

'It's Mrs Rivers's first King's Lynn, and she's only come because of you!'

'Well, that seems very flattering,' I said, reaching for the book.

'And I've had to persuade her to come and talk to you, even so.'

'This is one of those places where persuasion seems to work rather well,' I said, wondering if what was meant as a tribute didn't sound a bit like a rebuke. But there I was. I wasn't going anywhere. I was ready to be politely interrogated. The committee-member moved away, leaving Mrs Rivers alone at my table in what I took to be her shyness.

'Can I personalise it for you, or is it perhaps for someone else?' I asked, before signing it.

'You can just say "To Margaret", if you like,' she replied, with a twinkle.

I started to write 'For Margaret', believing that preposition to be the important distinction between the bestowal of a copy and a unique dedication, and somewhat disliking my own perhaps ungenerous pedantry at the same time, when she suddenly burst out with an unlikely accusation:

'You don't know me, do you?'

'I don't think so, no,' I said.

'Of course, why should you recognise me?' She laughed, rather as a guest at a party might laugh if the waiter filling up glasses had unaccountably passed her by even though her own was eagerly held out.

I paused, with my pen above the page, now feeling foolish. I looked at her again, as though recognition might suddenly arrive to save me from further accusation and her from further floundering. But all I saw was a presentable grey-haired woman in informal if expensive linen trousers-and-top with a scarlet scarf and an oddly military handbag , who was far from floundering. Nor was she shy. She seemed simply to be amused.

'You could perhaps sign it "Johnny"', she said finally.

Since my immediate thought was that I had never signed 'Johnny' to anything at all for possibly the whole of her life-time, I let my pen-holding hand hang down by my side.

'What is all this, then?' I asked, with as neutral a smile as I could muster. What was I missing? Where was this going?

'I'm Margaret,' she said, unnecessarily, I thought, since she had seen me write her name. 'I can't stay now. You're all being whisked away to the party, I've been told, and I have to get back this evening. But I hope you'll call in on us tomorrow. Runcton St. Peter is on your way home. Here's the address and directions. Please do. Please do, Johnny.'

She looked directly and earnestly at me as she handed me a piece of folded deep blue paper, and suddenly the force of the coincidence hit me, and I knew what she was going to say next.

'You remember, really, don't you?' she said. 'It was a very long time ago, and yet not such a long time ago when you think about these things. I think about things a lot these days. Yes, I'm Margaret Arne. Margaret Arne that was, as they say. I've been Margaret Rivers for my significant life. But I am also my father's daughter, whom you'll remember.'

I couldn't think of what to say.

'Margaret,' I said. 'Of course. Yes.'

'So you'll have to come, won't you? You could be with us by five o'clock. Five-thirty, maybe? One for the road? Yes.'

This was spoken by someone whose 'significant life' had been spent getting her own way, I thought. But now that I knew who she was, I could hear quite clearly in her commanding tone of voice the little girl that she once was and that I had known. There was nothing I could do but sign her copy with as convincing a 'Johnny' as my hand could manage (not very convincing at all) and promise to call on her when the festival finished on the Sunday.

She left the hall without delay, walking decisively to the exit, speaking to no one. I wanted to have told her about the CD I had found little more than two months before, and to share the coincidence with her. I wanted to ask her about her father. Could he still be alive?

I unfolded the paper she had given me, and read the address given in her soft ultramarine handwriting that was barely darker than the paper. It wasn't really on my way home. I would have to turn off towards Downham Market. But if I left King's Lynn in good time and was prepared to get home late, then I would have every opportunity to ask her whatever I liked.

2. A Frog to Storks

That bare description of the movements of the Arne piano concerto had brought back to me vividly one of Maurice's eager but stumbling explanations of it, long ago, given freely when in unguarded moments he could be induced to think of it at all.

'You see, Johnny, it's more of a monster than anyone suspects. I've been quite inconsiderately morose and self-pitying for two longish movements, so that when the scherzo comes along the listeners are all quite cheered. They think it's all over in a burst of optimism, tap their programmes on their knees, start to feel in their pockets for their cloakroom tickets and so forth.'

Here came a short pause for the famous Arne look, a cross between a surgeon's glare and a conjuror's roguishness.

'But no! there's another movement! The longest one of all, full of agony and all the answers to agony I can find it in my heart to propose. That hammers them back into their seats, I can tell you, the fools.'

After self-revelations like this he would lean back in his chair, feeling in his own pockets for something that might equally release him from something too painful to contemplate, his pipe perhaps.

Did he know then that I'd not yet properly heard the concerto? The young are very good at concealing their ignorance. After all, they have spent their whole lifetime so far doing exactly that. And in any case, everyone 'knew' Arne's concerto from *Missing in Moonlight*, starring Stewart Granger and Patricia Roc. It was the best thing in an otherwise rotten film, the one where Granger is a pilot managing to spend quite as much time writing the concerto as fighting the Germans, and doing both pretty well, whistling the last bits of it to Patricia Roc, who plays a WAAF ops-clerk trying to guide his shot-up Spitfire home. Arne hated the film, even though it had made him rather famous.

'It's twaddle, really,' he said. 'They even bothered to re-orchestrate it, so that it would sound a bit more like Eric Coates than me. And can you believe in Stewart Granger as a composer? I mean to say.'

I, of course, in my complacent knowledge about films, would have reminded him that Granger had played the lead in a film about Frederyk Chopin. But that simply reinforced his point. You couldn't believe in Stewart Granger as Chopin, either.

'I pinched the idea from Tchaikovsky, by the way. That march in the Sixth Symphony that almost has the audience rising from their seats? Then quite unexpectedly the true last movement, with those savage descending strings. Utter pathos.'

I wasn't sure what I really thought about pathos in music, or in anything else for that matter. My tastes were very different at that time. In my most intolerant moments I might have thought it 'pathetic' in that vernacular sense sometimes applied to Tchaikovsky's *Pathétique* itself. But truly I was impressed by Arne's high public profile, still not faded from view. I understood the privilege of hearing his views.

This was in 1956, nearly ten years after *Mission in Moonlight*, when I was in the RAF myself, doing my National Service, with nothing more dangerous asked of me than to guard the camp against attacks by the IRA, armed with those most effective weapons: red armband, whistle and stick. When I told Arne such stories, the comedy was not lost on him. Inclining his head gravely, he would say: 'Leading Aircraftsman Fuller, civilization is in your hands.'

Sixty years ago! It seems in some ways even longer than the 200 years that take me back to the Regency of my current researches. Arne himself could not have been much older than 40 then, probably younger. I was 19. I would be hard put to explain why he should have been interested in me and my doings, but the appearance of interest, in all its kindly circumstances, never wavered. And for me he was absolutely the centre of cultural activity in the leafy desert of Gloucestershire in which I found myself, and I never once questioned his hospitality. My life was suspended, much like a prisoner's, and something was needed to make my time go by. I did not know then (and perhaps have never fully known since, as none of us do) that this is the most wasteful and wicked treatment of time imaginable and comes of acting on the doubtful belief that the future may be of a different order to the past. Simply to pass the time, to endure, to put off the possibility of better things, is to cancel one's whole engagement with existence, to find oneself struck out of the present moment, turned away with a considerate smile by time's unaccommodating secretary.

What should I have been doing, really doing, instead of fidgeting in my life's waiting-room? It's hard to say. We all find ourselves in such a place for long stretches, and the whole point seems to be that there isn't actually anything to do there at all. Nothing to engage with the present moment, only out-of-date print and a sense of vague foreboding. The Now which is our field of battle is somewhere else. Really, we should be out looking for it.

When I got back from the National Portrait Gallery on the day I discovered *Five Post-War Romantics*, the first thing I did of course was to look Arne up in Grove, but the information was scarcely more detailed than that given in the niggardly note accompanying the CD.

ARNE, MAURICE MACKENZIE (1918–). Composer and maker of experimental films. Born into a musical family (his brother Hugh is a teacher of the viola and plays in the Con Amore String Quartet; their grandmother was the contralto Clara Mackenzie, QV) Maurice Arne began writing music early, and his first compositions for piano were performed at the

McNaughton-Lemare concerts while he was still at school. None of his early works was published, however, and he first came to wider notice with his Piano Concerto, written for Clifford Curzon and first performed in 1946 with the London Symphony Orchestra, conducted by Sir Malcolm Sargent. The concerto was featured the following year in Thorold Dickinson's film *Mission in Moonlight*. Later works include Symphonic Variations for Piano and Orchestra, a Clarinet Trio, and several ballets, among them *Susanna and the Elders* (Sadler's Wells, 1950) and the film-ballet *Margaret's Dream* (1957). In 1944 he married Paula Dudley, elder daughter of Lord Tewkesbury. From 1962 to 1975 he was Associate Professor of Composition at Mapleleaf College, Vermont, and Director of the Mapleleaf Festival.'

I could make nothing of this. What I already knew or half-knew was not illuminated; what I did not know made no sense. I knew he had finished the film about Margaret. Indeed, I had seen it in what I had thought was just about its final form, and had helped him with it. I didn't know whether he had included me in the credits or not. But what music had he written since then? Or indeed had he made more films? What on earth had he been doing in America? I simply could not visualize him presiding tweedily over Mapleleaf in those years of protest, flower-power and be-ins. And what of the past thirty-five years?

Was it foolish, though, to suppose him still alive? My Grove was an old one, and the CD (brought out in 1995, I noticed) not to be relied on for any authority in not providing a terminal date. I was well aware from anthologies of poetry (some even compiled by me) that apparent longevity was nothing more than a mistake by the editor, or the natural delay in which biography takes account of ending. The new Grove would settle matters, providing either the evidence of a late flowering or more probably the finality of a date of death.

But why 'more probably'? Human life is brief enough, when you look at it straight, but in its actual course it can be persistently varied and extended. It can be like the weather of a remembered day, whose significant moments are crowned by the clouds accumulating above in the exact shape of one's sight of them, but then dispersing into transient and unobserved formations during the long hours of an afternoon. And it is at sunset that the clouds linger longest, when attention to them again seems to hold them still. Look away to the distracting business of one's life, and the sky is never the same, but stare at twilight to a streaked horizon and the suspension is magical. The day, we know, is dying, but not yet! That little dash in Grove, leading from the certainty of birth only to the uncertainty of the as-yet unknown, the unclosing closure of a merely conventional point, that second parenthesis, was a perpetual hope, a typographical immortality. Death always closes his book, but for a time his finger stays there, marking a place on the open page.

And Arne, who had seemed quite old enough to me in 1956, in his fame and his habits, and with an almost-grown child, would still only be—what? 98? A fine old age, and not now so very uncommon. I could imagine him feeling that he had reached it almost by accident, or by a masterly touch of fate, like the whole final movement that was not at all expected: 'A chance for something to be resolved, eh, Johnny? Time for something to be worked out?'

I was 'Johnny' to him because he had picked up my old name from Jack Clark, the family friend who more or less introduced us. Naturally as I grew older I had expected the diminutive to be dropped. At school I was a surname, something perpetuated in the RAF, with the added flourish of rank. Now here I was, in a kind of misunderstanding, being called 'Johnny' again. I was wary of it, as evoking the worst of 'little Johnny Fuller', not sure that I could be a grown-up 'Johnny', slightly devil-may-care, but reliable in an emergency. It sounded raffish. Perhaps it seemed appropriate because I was in the RAF. I more than once felt that Arne unconsciously addressed me as the kind of airman I most certainly was not, bringing good cheer like a round of drinks, alert to the moment of duty, the careless hero. For my part, it took me some time to think of him as 'Maurice.'

He showed himself to be of Jack Clark's world by being in this way, as Jack was, a mythographer, casting his friends in the exaggerated roles that his dramatic sense of them required, worthy of the greatest awe and humour. Jack hit the tone perfectly in his thumb-nail sketch for me of the county environment my military service had accidentally engineered, as though simply by finding myself within five miles of 'the Dudleys' I could lay claim to their company. I had told him that I was posted to RAF Innsworth, and would be working in the accounts section. Jack's immediate presumption, correct as it turned out, was that calculation of the airmen's income tax would be much neglected and that I would find myself all the time at Charlwood with the Dudleys.

'Well done, my boy,' he said, with that little laugh of his, suggestive of collusion in a risqué adventure. It was a pleasant habit of his to treat me not as the young son of his friends, but as an honorary contemporary, free of their moral concern in which he need play no part. It was, I supposed, because he himself had first known my parents when he was a young man of my age, and had been content to maintain that relation. I in my turn had simply caught up with him. My father, I now see, may have thought that Arne was a dubious and bohemian influence (though he would never have offended me by saying so) and my mother, I am sure, thought that time spent at Charlwood was frittered away when I could just as well have spent week-ends at home in London.

Jack's view of me (as opposed to the more conventional parental one) was a distinction not only privately conferred upon me, but somehow communicated to Maurice and his wife, so that from the beginning I was received as a person in my own right, and not as extension of my parents to whom favours might be done through kindness to me. And in any case it was, as Jack's presumption about my leaving my *carte de visite* suggested, always open house at 'the Dudleys'. This suited me fine.

Why he called them 'the Dudleys' puzzled me. They were, of course, the Arnes. But Jack, who had been at Oxford with Richard Dudley and had known his sister Paula before she married Arne, was inclined by this experience and by his intuition of the marriage, to discount Arne's authority in any area of life beyond that of his music. It was a kind of anthropological throwback, a matrilocal marriage. Paula had brought an ancient name to her wedding, and it was not going to be so lightly cast away by her friends. It had a solid sound, consonant with the name of the house she brought with her, and with the money that enabled it to be kept up. She was therefore the central power in the marriage, and Maurice simply an appropriated enthusiasm, not all that different from her buying a grand piano because it was somehow for her an appropriate cultural gesture, slightly tendentious in the land-owning world she inhabited, even louche, but evidence of a lively sense of culture. That was what I felt at the time. A simpler reason for 'the Dudleys', as I now see it, was that Jack presumed to think of the household at Charlwood as consisting principally not of Paula and Maurice, but of Paula and Richard, his friend and therefore entrée to the family. Richard lived with his sister because he had never quite lived independently, and could have what was almost a whole wing of their Regency villa without getting in the way.

But Jack was vague about the ménage, vague even in his promise to write to them to alert them to my presence in Gloucestershire. If I was alarmed by his hints of horses and servants, I was reassured by the likelihood of nothing ever following from Jack's introduction. It belonged, I thought, to the world of his social fantasies, where everything that was logical, possible, convenient or desirable might be speculated upon, even promised, but would never actually occur. His conclusion ('Maurice will get you into films, dear boy') actually made me laugh. I was a military conscript, with the challenge of university to follow. How could I possibly, despite the fact that they were my passion, get 'into' films in the sense intended? I classed it as a Jack fantasy, along with a possibly more challenging remark which he let fall with, I thought, some care to avoid the innuendo that it undoubtedly contained: 'Paula will like you.' Such a thing is not said with the implication that one is the sort of person that not everyone will like (that is to say, 'Paula, at least, will like you'). Arne would surely have to 'like' me if he were to drive me, as I faintly pictured it, to significant lunches at Ealing Studios. Their daughter Margaret, who, I gathered, was neither quite a child nor quite grown up, might 'like' me or not at her whim, and the possibly simple or mad brother Richard need not 'like' me at all. But there was something in 'Paula will like you' far beyond the gracious acceptance of a hostess, a passport to meals and lifts and invitations. And that something, I feared, was sex.

In Jack's imagination, as I now see it, I was an innocent young protagonist from an early novel by Huxley or Waugh, unequal to the world's duplicities, slightly dull, and with a devotion to something high-minded that would become an inevitable ground for comedy. And I was to be thrown to the English eccentrics, like a frog to storks.

3. An old-fashioned Dadaist

National Service in the RAF was a distraction from my real life not quite interesting enough to be a true distraction. Years later I was amazed to discover that there were people who had actually managed to avoid it, and I therefore, so as not to seem unresourceful, came to pretend that it was some sort of adventure that I had welcomed and that had been good for me. Certainly I was unusually fit after two months of basic training, woken at 5.45 am and kept active until I simply fell asleep out of sheer fatigue at about 9 pm, with my boots on. A perfect regime for muscle, and for the digestion, inflicted upon us at Hednesford, near Cannock, by brooding corporals whose job it was to abuse us and to find things for us to do even if there were nothing to be done. Between spells of drill, and carrying large quantities of soap from one store-room to another, I read Arthur Machen and tried not to be noticed. Since I soon found myself friendly with a half-Polish art student called Cupid, possibly the most rebellious and cynical of my fellow conscripts, this wasn't always possible.

At Cardington, the camp near Bedford where we had enlisted, he had already smuggled in three girls, together with a writer friend called Holden, who asked me to give him some poems for a magazine. I was flattered by this, but I don't think I ever gave him any.

Two of the girls were too dirty to be interesting, and the third was bespoke. Soon the two dirty girls went off together, easily bored. But the rest of us would gather in Cupid's billet for illegal breakfasts of bread and treacle. Cupid would have his arm draped over the third girl's shoulder as though they were sheltering from a downpour. He talked about her impersonally as though she were a pet or a hostage.

'Can someone look after her today?'

'Sorry, I'm on guard duty.'

'Sorry, no can do.'

'Send her home.'

'We could keep her with us, couldn't we?' said Cupid. 'What about that coal shed at the end of the billets?'

'Or under the floorboards,' said someone, remembering films of prisoner-of-war camps.

'She's going to be found sooner or later,' someone else objected.

The girl stared with tight lips at the black nails of her hands held up in front of the stove for warmth. She certainly wasn't going to spend any time in a coal shed. She turned to look at me, as though I might hold the key to her future in some way, far from the idiocies of these conspirators. I gave her a rueful smile, admiring the straight line of her nose.

Cupid sighed. She was a fine trophy, a perfect symbol of his truculence and dissidence, but he was forced to agree. She left soon afterwards with Holden.

Cupid was a focus of discontent. He would have liked to see himself as a leader in the Warsaw uprising, emerging from a sewer in dark glasses at a crucial moment, brandishing a sten gun. But I thought that our plotting round the stove was more like Stalky & Co than a resistance movement. Our next task, in the perpetual hunger that seemed to afflict us, was to befriend a cook in the nearest cookhouse, who could wangle fried eggs by the dozen, making them into sandwiches that he hid in his battledress. Once I realised that I was going to survive it all, I could enjoy hating the RAF and passing muster.

Machen suited my mood: 'And every day we lead two lives, and the half of our soul is madness, and half heaven is lit by a black sun. I say I am a man, but who is the other that hides in me?' I had thought Machen a writer of fantasy adventures like some of Stevenson's; now I could see that he was like Kafka, whose diaries I had also started to read. I could even begin to relish the circumstances of enslavement. They suit a certain sort of adolescent melancholia. My French pen-friend Dominique referred in her letters to her perpetual 'cafard', a state I knew to be largely self-induced: it made her feel interestingly like Juliette Greco. To have real reasons for a 'cafard' was to be truly more interesting. (Dominique and I met on occasion, since she came to London, but preferred our letter-writing characters as, I suppose, better able to reveal our true selves to each other. I never went to Orléans).

All the same, I couldn't pretend that I was as interesting as Cupid, who was probably not going to survive it at all. At the eight o'clock parade, after more than two hours of breakfast, kit-polishing and room drill, he would still not be out of bed. When the duty corporal struck open his locker with a baton, dirty shirts would tumble out of it, like a drunken man who had fallen asleep on the other side of a door. He was almost perpetually on a seven-day charge, never quite shaven, wearing a smile of amused apology. The thrust-out lower lip, slightly raised and flattened, the half-lowered eyelids, seemed to say: 'Take me as I am. I can be no different.'

After basic training, and before Pool Flight, where the nature of our twenty months of real service was finally settled, we all had a couple of weeks of leave. We took the train from Brindley Heath, via Birmingham, to Euston and the mother of cities. There we could for a time exchange the deceptive anonymity of our uniform and number for the real anonymity of the face in the pleasure-seeking crowd, moving between the familiar stopping-places of our personal maps,—for me, the British Film Institute, the Hampstead Everyman, and the Chinese restaurants of Gerrard Street. It seemed a particular sign of high culture that there could be freely available desirable food other than treacle or fried-egg sandwiches. I think that all of us had been infected by the collective mentality of camp deprivation. Witness our ambivalent pleasure at a surprise inspection by the Catering Officer: 'Awful! Throw it away! Don't give them that. Look! it's all fat!' But we asked to have it anyway, because it was no worse than usual.

London pleasures were not all solitary. There were girls to take out for the evening, over-ceremoniously and with a dismal-comic sense of the unlikeliness of informalities after the formalities. When called-for, they would turn out to be nervously overdressed; when deposited at their homes they would have become, however fetching their physical presence still, enveloped in their tediousness like a cheap perfume. I remember one of them to this day. She was only about five feet tall. I could think of almost nothing to say to her that she might be interested in, and as we stalked down Shaftesbury Avenue my eyes were locked not to her over-powdered face but to her little half-bare bulging bosom, proud in the savage constraint of a low-cut gypsyish corsage. Was it my imagination, or did the face-powder shake free in little clouds at each sharp step of her high heels? And was she carrying a shiny handbag? And was she only about seventeen? I can hardly bear to think of the pathos of such rituals of over half a century ago.

In those days, although I wrote a lot of poetry, I was much more interested in films. The best that poetry could do, in my opinion, was to work quietly away inside the head like a miner in a cave, exposing unlikely seams. When something interesting was going on in the imagination, all that words could do was describe. I had found some copies of Roger Roughton's little magazine *Contemporary Poetry and Prose*, which had established a viable English forum for surrealism in the 1930s. He had published together William Empson and Dylan Thomas (more like each other than anyone else had realised), scenarios by Dali and Buñuel, Inuit legends, and French poetry translated by himself. I followed some of this up. Paul Éluard I found particularly mesmerising:

Le poisson avance
Comme un doigt dans un gant.

But even in the original it was still a kind of translation, the words transporting the conception clumsily across the grey yawning space between two minds. For a time I had thought of starting a magazine, and I roped in school friends whom I could publish and who would contribute five pounds each to the costs. But there was something about the magazine project that didn't ring as true for me as the making of films. A magazine was more like a way of energising friendship and the opinions and creativity of friends, whereas for me film-making was as properly solitary an activity as the writing of poetry, which it much resembled.

But films didn't need to be translated. They were immediate and tangible and multi-media. And they were the perfect embodiment of the surrealism that had become my passion. That was why I loved films.

I spent most of my leave with my film-editing splicer and the little bottle of film cement that smelled of nail varnish. The attentive excitements of this process had something weirdly erotic about them. If I had thought much about it I would have seen it paralleled in the typical spare-time activities of my contemporaries in the school prep-room: the cutting out of pieces of card with a razor, to make tiny fawn-and-cream Swiss trains; the toying over a chess-board with a predatory bishop; the filling of cardboard tubes with grains of nitrate. These toy symbols of power and explosions were a harmless sublimation of pubertal energies.

There were explosions in my current film, unusual noon fireworks saved from some reels taken in Rapallo, surprising disjections of the blue air into grey splashes and corkscrewed plumes. I intercut them with real flowers, and with the spokes of a bicycle. The idea was to represent the seven deadly sins with freely-associating abstractions, each with its appropriate colour and characteristic images. My cutting was orgasmic and rapid, some strips of the 8mm film no longer than an inch, the smell of nail varnish very strong. 'Spleen' was already finished. This section was 'Pride.' I think I had long realised that I didn't really have the energy or inspiration to make the other five.

I became grateful that there was never an opportunity for Arne to see these films. I risked sending them off, in registered packets, to competitions organised by amateur magazines and festivals. Even when they were in my possession, they would be in London and not in Gloucestershire, and Arne didn't have an 8mm projector. When he made his films, he naturally worked in 16mm. His enviable Paillard-Bolex was often lying carelessly on his study desk, business-like black and chrome against old mahogany, or sometimes mounted on its tripod as if the section of the bookcase it faced were of immense potential significance, or, if it happened to be tilted towards the ceiling, as though he were compiling some infinitely patient study of the domestic habits of spiders.

I could talk about my films, however, and easily make them sound more worthwhile than they were. And usually it would be the next film to be made that would be really interesting. There was always a new idea, a new technique, or a new enthusiasm. For me, film seemed to be a potential rather than an actual medium, perhaps because (unlike poetry) there were fewer profitable models, or fewer at any rate that were easy to come by. And I was keen to define what that potential might be.

Arne always did me the favour of considering carefully what I had to say.

'Yes, yes,' he would say, slowly. 'Perhaps.'

This was the politest way he knew of being entirely negative. It meant that he knew I was talking tripe. If anything I had to say were worth engaging with, he would engage with it.

'Abstraction,' he would say, frowning. 'I can see that it's possible, but it isn't very human, is it?'

I didn't see why not. Music was abstract, after all.

He would rock backwards and forwards on the grass, clasping his huge knee with interlaced fingers, or kneel on the rug, smoothing it out on either side. His restlessness was a sign of his engagement.

'Music? Oh no, *surely* not? You'd want it to be purely form, would you? But it can't be. It's an essence.'

Yes, I said. Essence was what I was after.

'Well,' said Arne firmly. 'You'll have to make up your mind. An essence is a concentration of something, not its removal. Music can only be emotion in its purest form. It's a kind of language *for* those emotions. There isn't anything else it can be, is there?'

Whereas film—film is simply *saturated* with the world out there, the world that we experience. How can you abstract that?'

I didn't know. I didn't know at all, but I was gripped by the irrational excitements of montage and its creation of worlds that were not at all 'out there' in Arne's sense.

'Ah, Johnny,' said Arne sadly, but not without respect. 'you're just an old-fashioned Dadaist. What it is to be young!'

For me, film was an extension of poetry, which I had written long before I was given my little camera. For Arne, it was an extension of music, or perhaps more particularly of ballet, into which for some years he seemed to have been inveigled. He claimed to have come to film itself through first using it in a stage ballet about (God forbid, I thought, when I heard of it) the raising of Lazarus. The film sequences represented the *outre tombe*, the experience beyond experience, as I understood it, and they sounded distinctly Cocteauesque.

'Cocteau. Indeed,' said Arne, when challenged. If he was at all perturbed or discomfited by the revelation that I wasn't, in my bursting cinéaste's enthusiasm, going to allow him to get away with anything for one minute, he didn't show it. He even seemed keen to pre-empt my cruel pointing out of sources.

'You'll remember an earlier use of film ballet, I'm sure?' he went on. 'Satie's *Parade*, with designs by Picasso? The interval itself was a film, a bit relentless for the audience, don't you think? Designed to deprive them of their visit to the bar?'

I knew about *Entr'acte*, directed by René Clair. I had contrived to show it at the school film society, and remembered its great slow-motion chase sequence, all top hats, open motors and camels, with affection. I could have discussed the shots of the ballet dancer's skirts taken from beneath a glass floor as a form of abstraction. But I was beginning to feel that I had no need to show off to Arne, since unlike most schoolmasters (the natural recipients of point-scoring or ingratiation) he was a man who actually did things, who created art, and was famous. So I was ready to listen.

'Think of what composers could have done with film if it had existed fifty years earlier, as indeed it might.' (Arne would be lying on his back now, his heels scuffing the grass, his hands passing

23

repeatedly over his hair). 'Can you imagine film sequences in *Das Rheingold*? Debussy might have used them in *Pelléas*, of course.'

These were not works that I knew. I murmured assent.

'Cocteau is a great poet of the cinema, after all,' he said. 'And decidedly not abstract.'

I was at a disadvantage here, never having seen Arne's ballets. I really didn't care for ballet at all, because it seemed a perverse way of conveying a story, without words, and the music always seemed simplistically rhythmical and repetitive. His *Lazarus* sounded a bit old hat, anyway, like Vaughan Williams's *Job*, as I conceived it. And there was something objectionable about these biblical themes, something self-satisfied about making your characters cavort before God. Dancers were unnatural anyway, with their great white thighs and their bruised toes crushed into a hoof-like hardness. What was wrong with just having the film of Lazarus's Orphée-like experiences?

I knew the answer to that one as well: there was no equivalent market for experimental films. But ballet was fairly popular, a distinctly English thing. And there was every licence in it for the bizarre. Perhaps it was, after all, wonderful to have the opportunity to write one.

4. A Mere Bagatelle

I had finally met Arne in May 1956 at an evening of films presented in the Pittville Pump Rooms by the Cheltenham Film Unit. One of his own films was being shown, and as a local celebrity he was persuaded to come and introduce it. I had been too shy to act on Jack's inducement out of the blue, but on that occasion I did bother to make myself known.

RAF Innsworth was about half way between Gloucester and Cheltenham. There was nothing to do in Gloucester, and precious little to do in Cheltenham, either, so that the Film Unit was immediately attractive to me. It was something of a misnomer, however, being in essence nothing more than an amateur film society concerned mainly with such ad hoc technical experiments as providing a synchronised soundtrack by winding audio tape on to the same reel as the film. When I first went along in January, the CFU was meeting on alternate Thursdays. At the early meetings a final sound copy of *Regency Cheltenham* had been shown, and script conferences held for a summer production. The film was dire, but it was at least a 16mm affair with an optical soundtrack. I spoke out at meetings, in the hope that something exciting might be done, and made a thorough nuisance of myself. Then, usually in a gloom at the lack of response, I would go off to the coffee bar and have a Swiss soup and Vienna loaf for a shilling, using the tablecloth as my private desk for the evening. Coffee bars were a recent phenomenon, the coffee coming in Perspex cups, with brown crystal sugar to be sprinkled on. Espresso had not quite yet arrived.

The film show in May was a different matter entirely. Where the CFU had got hold of the films I have no idea, perhaps from the British Film Institute. Some of them, I now realise, may have been engineered by Arne in addition to his own. I thought that they could not be much to the taste of the kindly sound engineers and hobbyists of the amateur ciné world.

Arne's film was called *Symphonie Pastorale*, and was little more than a capering accompaniment to a piece of his for solo flute, a young girl appearing from shrubbery or hiding behind leaden urns, with a sad harlequin dogging her, and so on. The music gave it some charm, care had been taken over the costumes and the credits were enviably professional (I thought of my own indistinctly hand-painted titles, and resolved to do better). There was another dance film, by Maya Deren, in which a male dancer in studio tights whirled and leaped within the free space created by the camera, beginning one movement in an art gallery and completing it on the top of a cliff. There was a film by Stan Brakhage which barely had human beings in it at all, but which conveyed its brooding claustrophobia through attention to furniture and domestic objects which seemed in mysterious ways to reflect human attention, the rooms in which the camera prowled having, it would seem, been recently vacated. And then there was Sidney Peterson's *The Petrified Dog*, which bowled me over. Afterwards, when I found myself at last confronted by Arne and telling him who I was, I said as much, evidently with unexpected enthusiasm, for Arne threw back his head and released a barely-vocalised snort of laughter at the distant ceiling.

Seeing that I might have been abashed or offended at this reaction, he immediately took my arm and drew me apart from the group of people we had been talking to.

'My dear fellow,' he said. 'I'm *quite* delighted. I was beginning to think that what we had here tonight was a quite decidedly earthbound series of lead balloons. You can see, can't you,' (and here his voice descended to a confidential whisper, and he gripped my elbow) 'why the heart positively sinks at the prospect of such an evening with the good burghers of Cheltenham. Why don't they stick to golf?'

'I liked your film, too,' I said, somewhat insincerely. But in truth I admitted to myself that it was a grown-up achievement for a man with a recognised career elsewhere, and I could acknowledge its careless ease, its confident sense of knowing just what it wanted to do.

'A bagatelle, a mere bagatelle,' said Arne.

He was a tall man, whose nervous gestures were accompanied by much evidence of arms and legs, of forward motions of the elbows or occasional raising of a knee. He had a shock of dark wavy hair that was in need of being thrown back from his forehead or tucked behind an ear, and his linen suit was a little grubby. He favoured pale clothes, and loose shirts with narrow pointed collars, of a kind that I had never seen for sale. I suppose after meeting Arne I must have looked for them, in the hope of improving my own appearance. My blue uniform shirts came with detached collars, as indeed had my white shirts at school, a tradition enabling both an economy in laundry and the starching of the most visible parts of the shirt. It left me, however, with an adam's apple permanently bruised by the front collar stud. I once complained of it to Arne.

'You'll have to be proud of it,' he said. 'Think of it as a mark of your profession, like a miller's thumb or violinist's neck. Or try a different size in shirts.'

Arne was often facetious about my 'profession', as though I had chosen it after long and careful consideration. I didn't know whether to find this encouraging or irritating. At our very first meeting after the film show, when we had left the Pump Rooms in a small group and drifted to a hotel for a drink, he asked me what I was up to at Innsworth. I told him that I was an accountant.

'Jack said you were going to learn Russian so that they could turn you into a spy. Much better to be an accountant, I would think.'

I tried to explain that I had indeed been allotted the trade of interpreter, but on my return from leave after basic training had

27

simply been sent to Innsworth as a pay clerk. I thought perhaps they had discovered that my father had been a member of some suspicious left-wing organisation in his youth.

'I'm afraid that would be giving them too much credit for intelligence and organisation,' said Arne. 'More likely to be a bureaucratic cock-up.'

It was true that there was one Leading Aircraftsman in the Accounts Section who had been going to be a radar mechanic, but no doubt that was also a sensitive occupation during the Cold War. Arne didn't seem to think my position at all ignominious.

'A very safe choice,' he insisted. 'And you'll have more time for writing.'

He was already organising another round of drinks, and I had time to take in the other members of our party. I knew the secretary of the CFU, who sat in a faintly smiling silence, having obviously hated the entire evening. And I knew Peter, the most intelligent and interesting member, an aeronautical engineer who seemed little involved with the actual affairs of the unit, but who turned up regularly to cast a critical eye over things.

The others were younger, and looked like students, vaguely attached to Arne: two young men called Mike and Denis, almost indistinguishable except for the colour of their ribbed jerseys, and a woman called Magda who I suddenly realised, when she stopped laughing and flirting with Arne and looked soulful for a moment, must about five years ago have been the wan Columbine of the film we had just seen. Her blonde hair was now scraped back and pinned in an awkward bun, but wisps of it framed her face, giving her the look of someone designedly lost in the melancholy spaces of her own life. Her face seemed fuller, and also blotchy, as though she was in the habit of savaging it in self-torment. I supposed that in the film she had been wearing the dead-white make-up of the Commedia dell'Arte (a fatal influence of *Les Enfants du Paradis*, perhaps, which I had disliked) but she was certainly not now the fey wraith she had once been. Arne was more than tolerant of the attentions she paid him. The wordless way in which he placed before her a fresh gin and tonic seemed to betray an intimacy.

Denis was still going on about Arne's 'bagatelle'. I thought him too sycophantic by half.

'It was like the stage bits of that film *Les Enfants du Paradis*,' he said. 'About the mime.'

Quite, I thought to myself. Not a strong recommendation.

'Debureau,' said Peter, helpfully.

'No,' said Denis. 'It was Jean-Louis Barrault, wasn't it?'

'Playing the part of Debureau,' said Peter.

This wasn't going to be a profitable conversation. Peter knew more about French cinema than most people I had met. His great passion was Renoir's *La Chienne*, a film I had never seen (and have never since seen), and he also admired Arletty, whose attractions as an actress I had never been able to understand. He could cope with the obtuse Denis.

I wanted to talk about *The Petrified Dog*, but Arne was being quietly diplomatic with the secretary a little out of earshot, and Mike, who appeared to be listening to Denis digging himself further and further into a hole over *Les Enfants du Paradis*, wore an expression of timid but studied attentiveness that I couldn't really interrupt. I looked at Magda, who was, I thought, acting the part of being ignored by Arne. If she had wanted to talk to me, she would have said something, I felt. Still, I embarked adventurously on a conversation. I somehow managed to convey the fact that I wrote poetry and made films, as though this might lead easily into a profitable discussion of such things, which were, after all, of the moment.

My heart sank as she turned her gaze upon me, piercing eyes the colour of bluebells, the high cheek-bones that seemed to narrow them, the poor skin masked by face powder, the long upper lip. She considered me carefully, in apparent torment, and then briefly touched my jaw.

'But you are so young,' she said. Her voice had the trace of an accent, which gave this unwelcome remark the effect of a quotation. What on earth did the 'but' mean? She knew nothing of the mature achievements that I had in mind, as yet unachieved. I had no reputation. I was certainly young, and surely painfully so, even if I did not acknowledge it. The 'but' simply had nothing to contrast with. It pretended to sound wise and elegiac, as though she practised such unanswerable pronouncements every day in private and had a store of them to come out with at suitable moments.

I almost laughed. It would have defused this moment, where I was put out and likely to remain so, by acknowledging what I decided must be a joke or an allusion. I thought of being on the West End stage, in a play by someone like Terence Rattigan. There I would indeed have given a brief and knowing laugh and leaned over to flick my lighter against her expectant cigarette. An allusion? What could it have been an allusion to? A film, perhaps. Some sophisticated 1930s comedy? We were drowning in films.

All I could think about was the helpless vertigo of sexual magnetism, the sense that nothing mattered but the falling release into the face of another person, that happy swoon compelling an intimate but daring contact. My own mouth seemed to ache at the relatively brief distance of hers. Her fingers at my cheek had sent a trail of sensation down my neck and across my shoulder as certainly as if they had continued along that path in reality.

I was sharply aware, of course, of her body as it had appeared in Arne's film, the corset tight over her ribs but with trailing laces, the nipples showing like bruises against her flattened chest, the ballerina's collar-bones, hands extended, palms downwards and shaping the air as if to convey motion in stasis. Here in the hotel bar this body was entirely hidden. The voice, tired, husky, insistent, had to do duty for it, conveying its contrary motions of attraction or repulsion. She continued, in this affected Garbo croak:

'You have it all before you, everything! Don't spoil it!'

I did laugh at this, and the sexual moment passed. I thought her presumptuous and might have said so if I could have found a way to acknowledge the liberty she had taken. It was easier to decide that it was all a well-meant piece of theatre, and when she knocked over her glass a moment later I could safely consider her merely drunk.

I had the sense that she was quietly taken in hand by Arne, helped to gather up her things, spoken to kindly and taken on her way. Arne had the knack of controlling gatherings like this, and the evening was wound up as easily as it had begun. Even the secretary seemed happy enough as we stood about on the pavement outside the hotel, making our farewells. Whatever he had thought of the films, he was now somehow convinced that the evening had been a success.

Arne said to me:

'Look, you must come over to Charlwood. Come to lunch on Sunday. Just the family,'

He thrust scribbled directions into my pocket. I felt dismissed and didn't linger. I refused an offer of coffee from Peter and was the first to head off towards my bus. As I left, Magda called after me:

'Goodbye! Don't be so solemn!'

She stepped into the gutter by mistake, and stepped back again, waving a little wave as though her hand was pinned to her shoulder. I waved back, with the generosity of someone released from an awkward situation. She was two feet from Arne, neither of them yet having made a move, though the others were already making their several ways down the street.

I thought of what Jack had said about Arne's concerto: 'Oh, that wonderful concerto! So wasted in the film, in all its English decencies. He wrote it for his student, you know, a grand passion. Then it has to be tidied up into pathos and heroics. Well, it's what the English seem to want.'

I thought that the 'bagatelle' *Symphonie Pastorale* was tidy enough in its way, a piece of English bucolic a bit like sanitised Sitwell. I didn't quite yet know what to make of Arne, but there was certainly something going on beneath the engaging and untroubled exterior. Did they, as I imagined (the impression as forceful and as naturally observed as if my back were not decisively turned on them), now face each other, as if to acknowledge that they were, for the first time in a long evening, at last alone?

5. A Pig in a Drawing Room

I escaped from the camp whenever I could, in the civilian clothes that we were allowed to wear outside. Despite its size, Innsworth was touched with the qualities of the country it disfigured: peaceable light, birds singing, a fresh smell,—except within the billets, which smelled like an ironmonger's. It often seemed to have rained, or to be about to rain. My choice of clothes was donkey jacket and pacamac, or raincoat and cap. I must have looked like a village lad, waiting for the bus, but to myself I was a doomed isolate. I imagined wearing dark glasses as a disguise. The supports, as in a passage in Kafka's *Diaries*, would not rest upon the ears, but actually enter the cheeks. I decided that I would use this as an image in a film. At the same time I thought of writing a short story which would be in the form of diaries like those of Kafka, mixing real events with dreams and philosophical truths.

At week-ends we could normally rely on 36-hour passes, occasionally 48s. A 36 gave me Saturday evening at home and most of Sunday, but the coach from the White City didn't get back to camp until after midnight. I had to creep into the billet, exhausted, to the accompaniment of the weekly Top Twenty which some of my fellow airmen might still be listening to. If any were, there was no point in turning it off. I would try to get to sleep in the only way possible, by identifying with the resolute or self-lacerating moods of the powerful vocalists then popular, Johnny Ray, Frankie Laine, Rosemary Clooney. I could pretend to be a drifter of the plains, tugging my blanket a little tighter about my shoulders and howling out a love-lorn wretchedness to the stars. However, in the course of the year a new kind of music began to hit the charts, not tearful but defiant, not sentimental but sexual. The difference was at its clearest in black music, which engineered the whole project of rhythm-and-blues; between, for example, the sweet harmonies and stoical regrets of the Inkspots (who had quite promisingly soporific qualities) and the shrieking violence of Little Richard (who abolished sleep for ever). It was no good consoling myself with my preference for Little Richard: I started the week badly, in a jangle of nerves. In any case, I would rather have had the Modern Jazz Quartet, who of course were not popular at all.

A weekend invitation from Arne conflicted with my desire for a general escape, but it promised pleasures enough, and what's more they would be pleasures ready to hand. They might well be a fair substitute for the long haul to London.

Arne seemed to be aware of this, for one of the first things he asked me when I arrived was what on earth I found to do with my spare time, always supposing that I had any of it. I had found my tortuous way from the bus, asking for help at a pub, disbelieving the size of the front gates, walking up the drive, ringing the bell in a white portico with clipped bushes in damaged urns on each side. I had been greeted by a grey-haired woman in an apron, who quickly beat a retreat. And now Arne was leading me into their drawing room and pouring me a drink, much as might have been done a hundred years before for the village curate, out of mixed piety and social duty. I could imagine the doctrinal platitudes diffidently offered in exchange for the squire's hospitality, and the squire in return making sure that he had all the answers ready. Now, of course, these roles were no longer possible. One couldn't even claim an ironic reversal. In a world where art had replaced religion, the relationship was no longer that of master and servant but of master and apprentice, and country houses were no longer the centres of estates, but had become salons.

'Why we need such large forces in peace-time is beyond me,' he laughed, wielding the gin bottle. 'You can't have very much to do.'

I took the glass, which was twice as heavy as I expected it to be, and contained the twin luxuries of ice and lemon. What was I to say? The acceptable answer (the one acceptable to me as well as to him) would have been out of character. I certainly wasn't writing my novel in my desk drawer while Corporal Black was away at mess meetings. I hadn't succeeded in galvanising the boffins of the CFU into filming one of my ideas. I wasn't even catching up with my reading of the mediaeval poets or the minor Victorian novelists in preparation for Oxford. My existing projects were at a standstill. They were daydreams only. I was in my waiting room, in a limbo of continual procrastination. I was stultified and exhausted, succumbing too frequently to sessions with the billet's dude quartet of poker players, or visits to the camp gaff for deadly films like *Raising a Riot* (Kenneth More) or *The Angel who Pawned her Harp* (Diane Cilento and David Kossoff).

I wasn't going to admit any of this, and at that very moment I saw clearly that it was all wonderfully going to change. Arne was the precise and immediate example and encouragement that I needed. If he could be working on an opera, and be making films, and being stimulating to his students (and to me), all at the same time, as well as being a husband and father and paying his income-tax, then surely I could stir my stumps a bit? I resolved to make a beginning that very evening on my Kafka-diaries story: it would be narrated by a hideous circus freak.

I diverted his question, and made jokes about my chosen haunts, none of which was as grand as the George in Cheltenham (which I had never been to before the evening of *The Petrified Dog* and couldn't have afforded). My worst extravagance was blowing almost a day's pay on rump steak, stilton and black coffee at The Black Tulip. Usually I had something like onion soup and croutons at Prinny's Buttery, where I had to listen to the proprietor's stories about her white cat's 'flu. Clearly Dumas was preferable to the Prince Regent, but neither was in those days either as exotic or as upmarket as the names pretended.

Arne grimaced.

'This is where the bourgeois soul of Cheltenham writhes in its eternal torment,' he said. 'My private vision of hell is waiting for buttered tea-cake in Maison Kunz. Or perhaps,' he added wickedly, 'it has been overtaken now by that noisy Peterson film. Not terribly good for the nerves, wouldn't you say?'

I said that its great noise was one of the wonderful things about it. It was true, I thought. The nightmarish soundtrack underwrote and gave consistent force to the film's bizarre range of situation and image in describing in some archetypal way the violent banality of American life. I could see that it was diametrically opposed to the quaint prettiness of Arne's film and its measured, *Syrinx*-like score.

'What is *interesting*,' said Arne, with his admirable and friendly facility for granting a position with which he essentially disagreed, and taking the conversation further, 'is whether it was meant to be music or not.'

I hadn't thought of that possibility and wondered if it mattered.

'Well, it might change the way you hear it, mightn't it?' he said.

'I suppose it's just what it is, which it has to be anyway,' I replied, 'and you've no time to decide what it is. You just hear it, don't you?'

I was conscious of the lameness of this, knowing that Arne had some possibly interesting theory in mind.

'Don't you just, though,' he replied, with a laugh. 'It's amazing what you can do with a tape-recorder. Have you heard Pierre Henri? No? Great fun. Do you think if he'd had a tape-recorder that Vivaldi would have put real dogs and birds into *The Four Seasons*?'

'No,' I said, uncertainly.

'Right answer!' cried Arne. 'You score fifty points. Another fifty if you can tell me why.'

He was staring at me with a wild grin. For a moment I thought that he had said fifty pounds.

'Two reasons, perhaps,' he added.

I wasn't quite on his wavelength, but I was enjoying the conversation. I was enjoying my gin, too.

'Perhaps he'd have preferred to include a sermon by the Pope,' I offered.

Arne was even more delighted.

'Spoken like a true Dadaist! No, my reasons are much more obvious, one general, one particular. The particular one first. It's tremendously *clever*, do you see, to represent a barking dog with a repeated note on the viola. He wouldn't pass up an opportunity like that. The *general* point. Now I've forgotten what the general point was.'

He giggled and started to fill his pipe.

'Was it something to do with noise?' I asked, feebly.

'Good man!' exclaimed Arne. 'Of course it was. Yes, it's the difference between noise and sound. Sound can have significance. We can isolate it, identify it and interpret it. And music can, if it wants to, organise it. Music *is*, after all, organised sound. Noise is simply sound that we don't pay attention to. Music is sound that we do pay attention to.'

He may perhaps have used this aphorism before, but he was as pleased with himself as if he'd just come up with it, and turned his sucking on his pipe, as he applied the down-dragged flame from his match, into a gentle sound of self-approval, a kind of interrogatory humming, which he kept up until the flame had taken, whereupon the humming was lost in clouds of smoke, and he went on:

'What's more, that viola sounds more like a dog than the dog does himself. That's the beauty of it. Now what did old *Petrified Dog* sound like, eh?'

I conceded again that old *Petrified Dog* was very noisy, but that it was nonetheless exciting.

'It was all about American myths,' I said. 'I thought it created great tension, and mystery.'

'Mystery', Arne pondered. 'Indeed, indeed.''

'Perhaps it was also meant to represent the mind of the idiot.' The film featured such a role, a grimacing person who climbed and hugged a statue of Lincoln and later a stone lion (presumably a representation of one aspect of the title).

'The mind of the idiot,' repeated Arne. 'Quite so.'

He was now openly mocking the film but was doing it with so much of his own sense of fun that I didn't really mind. I rather wanted the film all to myself, and I certainly didn't want anyone else to explain it to me. It was enough that Arne could take me seriously and leave it at that.

'I didn't really understand any of it at all,' he said with a wistful matter-of-factness. 'But I'll tell you something. That bit where the girl climbs out of the hole? And starts making awful faces into the hub-caps of cars? I understood that, all right. I've got a daughter just like that. You'll meet her presently. Just you see.'

I did indeed meet Margaret, who had been out riding with her mother. They were pink with the exercise and wore clothes that seemed to have little buckles and loops here and there, residually symbolic of harness, perhaps, as though they might once have had to be attached to their mounts. They stood about in boots on the carpet, like soldiers of an occupying force who could presume upon free entry but had not been made welcome. I stood up to be introduced, but still didn't feel I had quite come up to their level of dress and exhilaration.

Maurice (as I now decided to think of him, and as he asked me to call him) stayed on the sofa, raising one arm in greeting as though he thought he had just seen an old chum on the other side of a field.

'I haven't looked in on Mrs B.,' he said. 'But judging by the frightful smells, our lunch is well on its way. This is Johnny, our resident Dadaist. Johnny: Paula and Margaret, as is quite obvious.'

'What's a Dadaist?' asked Margaret.

'Someone who loves his Dada,' said Maurice. 'You could join, if you like.'

'No fear,' said Margaret emphatically.

Maurice turned to me.

'Hubcaps,' he said enigmatically. 'You see?'

Paula sighed, and glanced round the room as if to make sure there were no members of the Resistance hiding there. She was a sturdy, handsome woman with a helmet of yellow hair, and her smile wore its conscious tolerance like an old piece of family jewellery. It was something that gave her moral distinction, but she reserved the right to lock it away.

'I've simply no idea what we're talking about,' she said affably, 'but never mind. I'll go and change. Is the Pig down?'

'Haven't seen the Pig yet, I'm afraid,' said Maurice. 'But the paper has disappeared.'

'Ah,' said Paula, with understanding, and strode off. Margaret lingered, looking at me.

'What is a Dadaist? Really?' she asked.

'Well,' I said. 'A Dadaist is someone who is happy to expect a pig in a drawing room. It doesn't put him off one bit.'

Chuckles from Maurice. I was encouraged.

'In fact,' I added, 'a Dadaist is exactly the sort of person who would arrange for there to be a pig in the drawing room in the first place. Several pigs, possibly.'

My pleasure in this confident repartee was short-lived. Really I had no idea how old she was, and I was treating her like a child, or at least the tone of what I was saying showed that I thought I was addressing a child. But her plaits, a deceptive indicator in any event, were clearly part of the equestrian rig, and I was beginning to notice (was I?) an undeniable little bosom surmounting the general chubbiness behind her tailored jacket. She looked at me blankly.

'You're talking utter balls,' she said, and left the room after her mother.

Maurice laughed outright.

'I do apologise,' he said. 'But don't mind her. She picks up her language from her mother, and doesn't usually know what it means.'

I said I thought I had got off on the wrong foot.

'Not a bit, not a bit,' he said. 'She's actually fascinated by you, and can't believe that you're not a pilot.'

'Oh dear,' I said. 'How disappointing.'

'I told her that you were a poet instead, a rarer breed, and more worthy of her attention. I think that might do the trick. Though it's probably not true. I mean, that there are fewer poets than pilots.'

'Probably loads more,' I agreed.

'Yes. Well, never mind. Both categories are only of theoretical interest to Margaret. She hasn't yet grown out of a deep attachment to her pony, although I do believe that she likes listening to Dean Martin. I'm making a little film about her mind at the moment, believe it or not. Just the sort of thing that would appeal to you, with your love of the inscrutable, the mind of the idiot and all that.'

I must have communicated an interest in this project, for he ended his quite incomprehensible explanation of it by saying that I could help him with it if I liked.

'Wouldn't Margaret object?' I asked.

'Not at all,' he said. 'I don't even think she knows about it. She doesn't suspect a thing.'

The Pig turned out to be Paula's brother Richard, rather older than she was, quiet and moustached. There seemed to be some sort of shadow over him, typified by his hoarding of the *Observer* in his room all morning and flinging it, inside out like a jersey, on the window seat, a first impression that signalled a less than friendly self-absorption. Or rather, the shadow seemed to be cast by him, on to others. I was later to discover that he suffered from recurrent bouts of depression and was surprised to learn that he actually had a job, apparently with a wine-merchant in Hereford. He had so much the air of being tolerated, and of having whims, that he seemed more like someone in care than an independent member of a family.

'Anything in the paper, Pig?' asked Maurice.

'Not much,' was the stolid reply.

'Oh, good,' replied Maurice. 'So it doesn't matter that I didn't get a chance to read it. Presumably all is rosy in Algeria, then?'

The Pig grunted.

'It's on the window seat,' he said. 'Look.'

He nodded toward the window seat, which was partly scattered with small chintz cushions and partly covered with rotting quinces, as though Maurice might have forgotten where the window seat was. I was amused at his 'Not much' since this was a weekend when the US Department of Defense was preparing further tests of the H-bomb on Bikini Atoll, rendering it unfit for habitation. Sunlight flooded through the glass, illuminating diagonal columns of dust. A white cat sat on the cushions, bobbing its head in the awkward effort to lick its own chest with downward strokes of the tongue. It paused, knowing it was being looked at, and closed its eyes in an ecstasy of repose and attention.

'It looks quite nice outside,' said Maurice.

'Now you notice it!' said Paula. 'It's been perfectly nice all morning. You men are absolute troglodytes.'

'I hope you don't include Johnny in that charming description,' said Maurice. 'He was probably on parade at dawn.'

'Not at the weekends,' I said.

'Jolly good,' said Paula, vaguely.

6. Siesta

Lunch was the usual exchange of mysteries and commonplaces and politenesses that occur when you visit a family for the first time. The meal was served by the heavy-breathing Mrs B., who had cooked it. There was also a young woman in attendance, who turned out to be Mrs B.'s daughter. I was still greatly embarrassed by the apparent requirement to ignore servants, since this was like taking roast potatoes from a dish held out by my own granny and saying nothing about them, or worse, hearing nothing about them. Yes, it was the silence of those paid to clean and feed the wealthy that disturbed me the more. Surely Mrs B. would have wanted to say: 'Aren't they nice?' or complained about the vagaries of the oven temperature.

The lunch itself was surprisingly commonplace, not at all the counterpart of the room we ate it in, with its gilded mirror, brown English landscapes, piles of new books with dust wrappers already torn, firedogs in the empty grate, a surprising orchid with a wing of blooms like flattened humbugs, and the civilised country smell of dust, and beeswax, and quinces. But there was wine, and I was, as I always seemed to be in those days, remarkably hungry.

'What *do* you do, then?' asked Margaret, apparently still disappointed that I wasn't a pilot, and implying that if I was not on active duty at week-ends, particularly at week-ends, then the island nation might fairly be considered to be in mortal peril.

41

My Innsworth life seemed impossible to convey in that gathering, in the ignominy of its functions and routine. I could have amused Mrs B. with an account of it, I'm sure, but those around me at table were from a different world entirely. Consider: Paula, quick and critical in manner, had perhaps ridden to hounds that very morning with Wing-Commander Wiggins, someone I'd already earmarked as a person who odiously rode to hounds; the Pig (as Maurice had tactfully intimated to me by way of warning before lunch) had had a 'bad war', quite possibly, and therefore humiliatingly, in that authentic part of the RAF to which I strangely did not belong; and even Maurice, my ally, the cuckoo in the nest, the dissident artist, was transformed in this company, at this very moment, into his devil-may-care alter ego, Stewart Granger, dictating from his blazing cockpit the immense melody which an invisible orchestra lifted and supported, as angels lift and support a marble hero on a tomb, until the closing credits.

How could I puncture the aura of this noble myth by picturing my life to Margaret? Would I say that I was acquiring great skill in computing the income-tax of those hordes of the RAF Regiment in transit whom we called 'Rock Apes'? Would I admit that I kept these accounts in large green metal boxes, each containing perhaps a dozen flat trays of accounts which pulled out from the front, each tray with about twenty individual accounts in multi-carbon form, fitting into plastic grips at the front indicating the airman's name? And that in answering queries at the desk outside the accounts room I would take the whole tray, with the individual accounts flipped back to reveal the one in question? And that I sometimes had to carry whole boxes of accounts, that felt as heavy as car engines, out to waiting lorries?

Where was the significant interest in recounting the typical problem or inquiry concerning the individual pay due, which was not being paid, and for which I would be blamed by the corporal or the flight-sergeant, or perhaps by Warrant-Officer Beacham, or even (God forbid) by Wing-Commander Wiggins? I had to be continually aware, in a multitude of cases, of all the qualifying allowances, depending on marital status or the nature of particular duties, and of all increases of pay due on promotion. Errors of calculation had to be identified at the end of each working day, when totalling all figures. We were given a machine about the size of a telephone, with an arm that had to be pulled forward sharply. These machines were without electricity, and must have worked on the same sort of principle as Charles Babbage's Analytical Engine of a hundred years earlier. From the little lists, printed on paper rolls, and torn off for scrutiny, we would discover whether or not our figures tallied. If we were 10/- out, the process must be gone through again. And again. Sometimes I would have to give up all hope of The Black Tulip or Prinny's Buttery.

Still, all life must be endured, and if it can be endured in a comradely spirit, so much the better. After an evening of desperate tugging at the arm of the Babbage machine, listening to the grating clicks of its cogs and springs, hoping against hope that it was actually accumulating a satisfactory answer to the problem that kept us there, it was a mindless relief to feed the stove with tins of floor polish and heat up a pan of chicken noodle soup into which we sliced bananas. Then poker, perhaps, or the quiet sewing of anodised buttons on to a greatcoat.

I could hardly conceal my occupation, but to speak in detail of such things would have been futile, as though the squire's daughter could have any real interest in the existence of a frame-worker or cottager on her father's estate. It had been presumptuous to suppose that I was even as interesting as a curate.

Above all, I would have liked to say such a thing, to have exposed my situation with a joke. It would have amused Maurice, at any rate, but looking at the other faces round the table I knew that it wasn't possible. It looked as though he had married into a stiffness of a kind that I already knew was not a part of his own character.

'I mean,' continued Margaret, 'what's the point of being in the RAF if you don't go in aeroplanes?'

'Well,' I said, truthfully enough, but ready for extemporisation, 'I was in an aeroplane last week.'

It had been a one and a half hour trip in a Hastings to Abingdon, for no particular purpose, except perhaps to give us a taste of what it was like to fly without stewardesses and little meals on trays, or, for that matter, without seats. We had staggered about the metal interior from one side to the other, trying to guess where we were, but for the most part able to see only clouds, laid out below us like a culture of penicillin. During the return journey we noticed that one of the engines had stopped. I told her all this as laconically as I could. I could see that she was almost satisfied. Particularly by the dud engine.

'But what was it for?' she persisted. 'What were you doing?'

'Ah,' I replied. 'I'm afraid I can't tell you that. It's a secret.'

She decided that she would have to be satisfied with this reply, which I thought in the circumstances was gracious of her.

'Yes,' she said. 'Daddy has secrets. But the great thing is…'

She lowered her voice in confidence, but since at that moment she was handed the apple crumble it wasn't likely that her words escaped notice.

'…anyone can have them, and I've got quite a few of my own.'

'Good for you,' I said.

A film of the 'mind' of this person would, I thought, consist very much of guesswork. But perhaps a father was much closer to his daughter than I generally supposed (or than the evidence of this lunch revealed in Maurice's case). Behind the affectionate insults was a long history of observed growing and shared activity: night feeds, sandy bathing dresses, shaken thermometers. Perhaps his film would really be a film about his own mind, just as the documentary I was planning about Blackheath and its self-absorbed inhabitants would be bound to reflect my own sense of dislocation or restrained violence.

I had no expectation of being able to make a real contribution to Maurice's film, but I hoped to be able to pick up some technical tricks. Most of the things that I didn't know were surely quite simple to discover. How could I hire a 16mm camera, for example, and where did you send negative film to be processed (my own camera produced positive film, and I was forced to edit the only copy)? How did you mark up a negative for optical effects such as dissolves? How to negotiate the minefield of a soundtrack?

The films I had made so far were silent. My excuse was the myth that the coming of sound had ruined the movies. The brief classics of the European avant-garde that had most excited me, like *Un Chien Andalou* or *Emak Bakia*, were soundless exercises in dream or shape. Even the longer classics of the silent era, seen in a school lecture-theatre or local film society, were accompanied only by the whirring of the projector which, since it was in the same room as the spectators, equally contributed its own intoxicating smell, that combination of oil, lamp-dust and heated celluloid that was a part for me of the ritual mysteries of film, like the incense of a shrine that induced visions.

After lunch, we wandered in the garden, which extended in all directions, including some further garden beyond high walls, orchard, some field and a stretch of river. From the distance of the garden, Charlwood achieved the full scale and presence among its small conifers and single hectic monkey-puzzle that so far had been concealed from me. I had seemed to approach it from the side, where Victorian additions and a decaying conservatory half hidden by rampant ivy gave it a misleadingly gloomy, even suburban, feel. From the rear, however, the white extent of the broad stuccoed masses, linked by classical cornices and by narrow balconies and half-roofs of green ironwork, marked it unmistakably as an elegant Regency villa. It needed a coat of paint, I thought, and some restoration of the ironwork, but this was not a period when old houses could be given the attention they deserved.

I was taken to see Margaret's pony, Danger, which she proposed to spend the afternoon grooming. I was relieved to find it a commonplace, irregularly-shaped animal of its kind, rather than some nervous glossy creature posing for Stubbs in accoutrements of black leather.

'Did you know,' said Maurice, 'that a horse is more expensive to maintain than a motor car?'

I said that I could well believe it.

We left Margaret and Paula in the stables. The Pig had returned to his room. There had been no question of clearing up lunch. Mrs B. and her daughter busied themselves with that, and were later to be seen in the vegetable garden, bent to their various tasks among the heavy rows. I wondered if they lived in the house or came up from the village, and if there was a Mr B. Perhaps he looked after the horses.

'Don't breathe a word of this,' said Maurice, 'but we had rather hoped that Margaret might be induced to give up the pony when she goes away to school next term. Just think of the animal quietly rotting away here for months on end while she discovers life's other little pains and pleasures.'

The school he named was familiar to me, a word connoting notoriety beyond mere educational theory of an enlightened kind, a name perhaps even suggestive of scandal. I remembered overhearing Jack talking to my father about it, as an establishment where the boys were allowed to smoke and to freely mix with the girls, 'chatting to them in their baths', as he put it, 'and flicking their cigarette ash into the water.'

I thought such vignettes stimulating, implying that sexual situations might be allowed to occur without anyone really acknowledging them or bothering about whether they would develop into anything, a delicious and ecstatic stasis of mutually agreed prolongation and deferral. Imagining Maurice's healthy daughter in that environment, however, was a different matter. Walking with him in the grounds of Charlwood, garden beyond garden it seemed, a place with its own protected freedom, I couldn't help thinking of the Spartan lack of privacy of my own school. Didn't girls after all need protecting from boys, from chilly rooms with bare floorboards, from steam and laughter and flicked towels, from the sight of their hairy genitals?

Margaret was a man's daughter, her features containing an elusive version of his own beneath the Dudley head and the florid fullness of cheek and lip that was the temporary badge of the age she belonged to, and I saw her with as much of a father's eye as I could imagine. How could he want to send her away? What torture of initiation did he imagine in that rueful phrase 'life's other little pains and pleasures'?

We came to a small paved garden between high walls, with beds of herbs planted in a maze-like pattern, rosemary, fennel, marjoram, all beginning to climb and throng in the liberty that the season accords to them. In the centre was a stone figure that I recognised.

It was a startled nymph, looking back over her shoulder and reaching forward into leaves. In a moment I remembered where I had seen it. It was in Maurice's film of the previous Thursday, centrepiece of the garden setting where the younger Magda fled for him through archways and peeped from bushes, her hands playing an imaginary flute, like the spirit of a grove. Seeing this setting in the heart of his little estate made me feel more than ever that Maurice had caught her in some way, that the film, far from being an afterthought to the score, the expression of a musical idea, as so much ballet clearly was, had been for him an excuse to capture the essence of Magda, something of her teasing and elusiveness.

'Daphne,' said Maurice. 'A copy of quite a famous one in the Uffizi and it's been here as long as the house. It shouldn't be outside, I'm afraid, and shouldn't probably be green. But I always think that's appropriate for a girl turning into a tree, if you see what I mean.'

I was stroking the rich organic patina on the surface of the calf and thigh. Maurice's black-and-white film hadn't, of course, conveyed the peculiarity of colour. He went on to explain.

'Daphne, chased by Apollo into a tree. I mean, she turns into a tree. Described in Ovid. She eludes him, but he gets the tree instead, by the handful. Leaves, do you see, the poet's laurel crown. Not the handful he would have liked, by any means.'

I looked at him and smiled. I was thinking of Magda as Columbine in the film, not being her own Daphne exactly, but offering herself as both subject and actor, ready to be made up, to be laced, to do whatever she was told to do. Was she not then his fantasy, his Coppelia? Had she not been wound up by him and set in motion, and weren't the clockwork springs still turning? Didn't he, in fact, have both his Daphne and his laurel crown into the bargain?

I thought, again, of what Jack had said about the piano concerto, 'written for a student of his.' Had it been a similar indulgence? I associated it in my mind with Alban Berg's Violin Concerto, as a work of pain and commemoration, but perhaps this was an illusion that owed too much to the particular story of the Dickinson film, with its noble deaths and stoical farewells. The concerto itself was in the untranslatable private language of Maurice's own feelings, and its conjurations needed no actors. But it needed its original subject, whatever that was, just as the god needed the nymph.

'Apollo as Harlequin,' I said.

'Absolutely,' said Maurice, looking at me sharply. 'The comedy of the eternal moment.'

I thought I detected a note of sombre reflection here, quite different from the expository manner of the host. He was used, perhaps, to showing people round, but not so often to talking about his work at the same time.

'It's true about comedy, isn't it?' he continued. 'It's our sense of the moment suspended, of life going on for ever.'

'Like the Forest of Arden,' I suggested.

'Exactly,' he said. 'For a space of time, nothing can be resolved. Hardships can be endured, and so aren't really hardships any more. Life is all beautifully open to a commentary on itself. Youth can admire itself. Love indulges its fantasies. Tomorrow is postponed.'

'There are no clocks i'the forest.'

'So true, so true. It's what the pastoral is all about. It's what my film was about.'

He paused for a moment, and then fired a question at me, as if to divert me from any further consideration of what his film was really about.

'Where does it come from, the pastoral? Why shepherds?'

It was half a genuine musing, half a schoolmasterly question. Was he going to award me fifty points again? And if I didn't have a good enough answer, would I have to give fifty points back?

'It's the siesta,' I said, quite on the spur of the moment. 'The Sicilian siesta in the heat of the day, the flock under the olive trees, and time stopped. The shepherd plays his pipe to his shepherdess.'

'Excellent,' said Maurice. 'Except that she isn't actually there. He plays his pipe and thinks of his shepherdess.'

As if on cue somehow, there came a raised voice from the kitchen garden behind us and out of sight. It was Paula's voice, insistent, reasonable, but slightly agitated and querulous. I couldn't hear what she was saying, but it sounded like a remonstration of some kind. Did it in fact come from the kitchen garden? Could she be tearing a strip off poor old Mrs B? My sense of the geography was a bit confused. Perhaps the voice came, after all, from the stables where we had left her with Margaret. That should have been more likely, though the stables felt to be in quite another direction. Whatever it was didn't matter much, but I thought to myself: she doesn't care about being heard, she doesn't mind being beastly to anybody, she certainly isn't aware of me or wanting to keep peace with guests in the house. It was revealing, somehow.

Maurice took no notice of it.

'Yes,' he went on. 'The shepherdess is somewhere else entirely. Probably slaving over a vat of cheese.'

We walked on through the garden fragrances. Was this last remark trying to tell me something? I was never sure with Maurice. He was infectiously eager for talk, wherever it might lead, but not unduly ready to talk about himself. At the same time, there was nothing disingenuous about him. He was someone who said what he meant and meant what he said. And yet again, he had 'secrets' which his daughter thought that she knew about. What on earth could that mean? Was he sending her away to school because she was getting to know too much for her own good? No, I must be careful not to get too melodramatic.

The day had certainly got warmer. Maurice had taken off his linen jacket and was carrying it over his shoulder with his finger in the loop at its neck. His trousers were, I noticed, held up by what appeared to be an old striped tie. There was an L-shaped tear in his shirt, like the turned-down corner of a book.

Somewhere in the distance, invisibly, as if merely enjoying the high blue sky, there could be heard the tiny insistent purr of an aeroplane, reminding me that my afternoon at Charlwood, like the amorous pastoral siestas of Theocritus, could not go on for ever.

7. Everything that Mattered

But these Sundays recurred, with open invitation and eager attendance, like a renewed faith. The little tinny bus, reeking of chrome and rexine in the morning sun, worked on my devotion like a tolling bell. The walk up from the village, with its one closed shop like an unconvincing detail of flat scene-painting in an otherwise startling mise-en-scène (earning a round of applause as the curtain rises on Act II), was a processional. My head supplied the music, and it was invariably Arne of some kind, because as well as the records I had hunted out at home (*Lazarus*, mainly) he had started to lend me things he had written for piano ('There you go, get your fingers into that—it'll be like kneading bread') and I would take them back to the NAAFI piano, which was available and deserted at certain times, very early in the morning, or on Wednesday afternoon, which was sports day.

Much of his music was too difficult for me, but like many amateur pianists I was never deterred by difficulty in music I was curious about, even sought it out simply to see how the familiar but mysterious or complex effects were produced. It was often a shock to see that (for example) a luminous melody with lucid arpeggios turned out to be written out over three staves in five flats, while a dense and furious passage of apparently clotted sound could be played with no more than two or three fingers of each hand. Anyway, if I had stuck to pieces I could eventually perform, life would have been much duller. The collection I kept at Innsworth consisted of war-horses I had long attempted, with mixed success, to thunder or blunder through. Khachaturian's *Toccata*, which the NAAFI piano rebelled against violently; Arthur Benjamin's *Jamaican Rumba*, which it was pleasantly seduced by; Debussy's *Doctor Gradus ad Parnassum*, which it couldn't cope with at all. The last of these I had watched a friend play at school, when he couldn't have been more than about fourteen, much too fast and with too much pedal, but with a persistent bravura (the lips meeting in an unaccustomed and wavering slit across his mouth as if to seal in with trembling compression the notes that were boiling in his brain) and this bravura had inspired me to try it, too. I had also ordered Shostakovitch's *24 Preludes and Fugues*, recently published, but not yet recorded. I found these severe at first, and brought them to Maurice, along with the second Piano Sonata, which I had similar problems with.

It might have been like confessing to a little difficulty with one of the Thirty-Nine Articles, to be discussed in a perfectly friendly way over a glass of Madeira with the Bishop. But Maurice was notably broad church in these matters.

'Ah,' he said, leafing through the music. 'A new kind of neo-classicism. But the Russians invented neo-classicism, so I suppose they must be allowed to go on doing exactly what they want.'

He sat down at the baby grand in the drawing room, and opened the *24 Preludes and Fugues* at random.

'There,' he said, 'do you see?'

His fingers walked and bounced on the keys like children amongst toys that they have no fear of breaking.

'He's been listening to Bach. He's been *bowled over* by the old juggler. Listen.'

Maurice wasn't an accurate sight-reader, by any means, but he kept going, at the right tempo, which is three-quarters of that particular battle I was always losing.

'What does that remind you of?'

He modulated without a pause into something of similar angularity and complexity that was, however, recognisably baroque, looking up at me with his expectant twinkle.

'All the voi-ces co-ming in!' he sang, keeping his eyes on mine, letting his fingers stumble for the approximately right notes on the keyboard. 'Ar-ith-meti-cal in-ver-sions! Re-pre-sent-ing God's three per-sons!'

He looked back at the Shostakovitch, managing a key change stiffly, but effectively, like a lorry-driver going up a hill, and then almost shouted:

'But what's this? Good Lord, it's the tremendous Slav soul breaking through!'

He exaggerated the yearning intervals of the fugue's theme, laughing happily until the music became too complicated, singing mad extra lines and collapsing with his elbows on his knees and his cheek on the keyboard.

'Hey! You're not telling me that you can play all this, Johnny?'

'I can play some of the preludes.'

'Quite so. Play what you can, of course,'

We looked at the sonata, which without hesitation he took at four times the speed I had yet managed. After a couple of breakdowns he kept going at a slightly more comfortable tempo, singing along with manifest pleasure.

'Ta-*tum*. Ta-*tum*. Tum-ti-*tum*. Tum-ti-tum-tum-ti-tum-tum-*tum*, ti-tum-ti-*tum*, da-le-da…'

He broke off, roaring with laughter.

'Alberti and a half, wouldn't you say? It's like Haydn, for God's sake! Russian heart-ache in the manner of Papa Haydn. Bit hard on the accompanying hand, though.'

I said that I thought some of the *Concerto for Piano, Trumpet and Strings* was like Haydn.

'Yes,' said Maurice, 'but that's such a bizarre mixture of things, isn't it? I think that Shostakovitch is really a very severe little man, tremendously hard on himself, always about to burst into tears, but torturing himself, simply torturing himself, into making all these dull jokes.'

He could see that I looked doubtful at this, and recollected that this was my music, that I had bothered to send away for and had brought to show him. He hastened to qualify himself.

'Don't think I don't admire him. I do, enormously. He's probably about the best symphonist there is. Better than Vaughan Williams. But very like Mahler, a great searching compendium of effects, a great economy of means, magnificent scale, all that. Do you know the Sixth? Yes, of course you do. Ridiculous structure, a Largo followed by two fast movements. Much the opposite of Tchaikovsky's Sixth, I suppose, a profound bleakness simply *brushed* aside with circus foolery. It works, though. My goodness, it works.'

We talked about neo-classicism, which I could see that he was uneasy about.

'I don't mind the pastiche, you understand. Art proceeds by affectionate imitation. But it's this pretence that the nineteenth century never happened at all, the idea that elegance and dryness are everything. It's nonsense, isn't it? What was the greatest invention of the nineteenth century? Culturally speaking, of course. I'm not talking about railways or anaesthetics.'

'Photography?' I suggested. 'Moving pictures?'

'Well, yes, of *course*,' laughed Maurice. 'You would say that, wouldn't you? But I was going to propose the symphony orchestra. We're talking music here, after all. The modern orchestra, in all its potentiality. Strings, woodwind, brass, percussion, infinitely augmentable, three harps if you want, piano and celesta if you want, Chinese gongs, sixteen double-bass, organ, choir, you name it.'

I protested that Shostakovich used all that.

'He does,' said Maurice. 'He's off the hook, I agree. Completely exonerated. And I'm not saying that elegance isn't also at times a virtue. It's the adoration of the infantile I'm talking about.'

He spun round on the piano stool and faced the keyboard again, his fingers picking out the sad little rising figuration of the second of Poulenc's *Mouvements Perpetuels*. He looked back at me over his shoulder as he played, exaggerating the flat effect of the repetitions and making a fastidious expression with his pursed mouth, as though the composer had made a nasty smell.

I almost hated him for that. The *Mouvements Perpetuels* were pieces I never got tired of playing, and I tried to say so. But Maurice was in mid-flow:

'Blame it on Stravinsky. Listen.'

He performed his gear shift again.

'*Les Cinq Doigts*,' he explained. 'Uncle Igor's five-finger exercises.'

He left the piano at that point. He could always sense the moment when I was going to prove to be not quite the totally tractable pupil he expected. It was the same moment that he remembered that I wasn't a pupil at all, and that too much demonstration might be thought, in what was nothing more than a friendly conversation, theatrical and counterproductive. He wound up his assault on Stravinsky.

'I simply fail to see why, after such a brilliant series of escape routes from the great cul-de-sac of Rimsky, not least the simply astounding barbarity of *Les Noces*, he decides that he wanted to sound like Pergolesi. And now (have you heard *The Rake's Progress?*) like Mozart! A sort of wincing, pickled Mozart at that. He even has recitatives, with harpsichord! I ask you.'

I had indeed heard it, in a recording produced in triumph from the States and played to a roomful of people who talked too much. I hadn't made a great deal of it, but what I'd heard I'd quite liked.

'And Poulenc got everything from Stravinsky, everything that mattered.'

As if sensing that he might now be challenging too many of my perhaps dearly-held assumptions, he steered me to the living room, where Margaret was lying in supine stillness on the sofa, as though about to be elevated by an illusionist.

I was thinking about 'what mattered.' You might have said that Maurice himself got everything that mattered from Rachmaninov, or perhaps even from Tchaikovsky, for these composers seemed to be his passions, unfashionable as they might have been among serious musicians at that date. It was something to do with the 'Slav soul' that he was always going on about. Sibelius, too, was frequently mentioned. There was a touch of frost in Arne, which often took you by surprise. The flute score of *Symphonie Pastorale*, for example, that could so easily have been like Debussy in classical mode, a pipe in sunny Thessaly, was a bleaker business altogether. The wind blowing across the mouthpiece of the instrument had come across ice and snow, and spoke sadly of them to the precarious spring of an English garden. It had fitted well with the famished look of Magda's shoulders and the way the bodice was drawn so tightly into her back and chest as though, revealing as it was, it had been laced up as a protection and not as a masquerade of the moment; and the movement of her fingers, warding off an enchantment, made them seem like something delicate, about to die.

Margaret looked up, from the solidity of her repose.

'You sounded as if you were having fun.'

'Well, that's not surprising, is it?' said Maurice. 'Music *is* fun.'

She gave a bitter laugh, and looked back at her feet. I thought this odd until I saw that she was in fact reading a tiny book, which she held at arms' length on her skirt. Was she long-sighted?'

'I think Mummy's made us all some coffee,' Maurice continued. 'Why don't you go and investigate?'

She looked up again and opened her eyes widely in an operatic glare. I thought for a moment that she was about to make some objection, but her face became slowly suffused with an utterly false smile, and she bounced out of the room.

'You can never quite tell what's going on inside that head,' he said. 'We might get our coffee, or she might have gone to jump hurdles. Music's a dangerous topic with Margaret. She had lessons, of course, and for a time I almost believed she enjoyed it. She got to the stage of rattling through "Pebbly Shallows" and "The Merry Peasant", and then that was it. She just didn't want to go on. Didn't see the point.'

I said that I thought it was a shame, but I couldn't tell how disappointed Maurice might still be that she wasn't interested in playing. Perhaps he was even relieved in a way, as if it pleased him to have confirmation of his daughter's utter indifference.

'I mean she *could* play,' he said. 'It was as though she was happy to demonstrate the ability, and that the ability gave her the right to assert the complete irrelevance of music. For her. She seems reasonably tolerant of it in others. Thank goodness.'

When Margaret came back with the full coffee tray, it was as an ambassador bearing some concessionary document that might be, or might not be, signed. I guessed that it was my presence that had induced her to play host. I couldn't imagine her doing it otherwise, with her ingrained habit of merely grunting at her father.

But the cat got in the way of her feet, and she dropped the whole lot on the floor.

These moments when they happen to us move out of the realm of sequential time. The unexpectedness of disaster compels the mind to withdraw and contemplate it from afar. There is an endlessness to what one sees oneself unavoidably doing, a series of snapshots of the irretrievable. But for the witnesses there is always a kind of pathos. Maurice was suddenly and uncharacteristically troubled and concerned, as though he were responsible for her stumbling.

'Oh, Puggins, sweetie!' he exclaimed, leaping up.

I thought there were tears in her eyes, not only of shock or hurt (she caught her elbow sharply on the edge of a table) but of shame at being betrayed in her momentary role of autonomous adult aware of the politeness due to a guest, and shame, too, at the consolation offered by her father in the form of a babyish nickname, which I hadn't previously heard, another sort of betrayal. It led her to refuse his assistance in dealing with the broken cups and steaming pool of liquid, so that he stood by awkwardly, oblivious of me, his hand going out instinctively above her in little actions that either followed her own in gathering the pieces or half-reached out tenderly as if he wanted to stroke her head and didn't dare to.

Later, as if himself embarrassed by his feelings, he spoke only of his regret at not catching such material on film.

'If only the camera could always be ready, and not need lights, ever! They should invent a kind of recording tape for cameras as well as for music.'

It was typical of him to turn the incident into a prophecy of the video camera. At the time I simply felt the stripped emotion of his uneasy fatherly feelings for his unmusical dumpling of a daughter. Was that all, really, that feelings were? The leftovers of unfulfilled relationship? The waste parts that it was mawkish to dwell upon? She had of course outgrown 'Puggins.' She was no longer 'Puggins.' But somewhere in his consciousness that was just who she was.

In the absence of coffee or any concerned appearance of Paula, and with instinctive respect for Margaret's dignified retreat, we returned to the piano next door. I was mindful of the wonderful way in which music can preserve the pathos of life's botched feelings and keep it pure and uncontaminated by bathetic detail like pieces of broken crockery. Music could certainly do it more efficiently than poetry. And I wanted poetry to be more like music.

There was pathos in the little pieces for clarinet and piano that he gave me to look at, too. They were like folk songs that had been broken up and reconstituted, as if by a scholar with an insufficient text but a generous breadth of musical understanding. The clarinet struggled for continuity of melody as if against some choking grief, while the piano simply put in chords and phrases here and there to establish a tonal argument that might go some way to explain the clarinet's piercing excursions.

The clarinet was Maurice's instrument, and it suited something bird-like in his bearing and character, a quality of stalk and pounce. When he played, the dark hair fell further over his face than ever, and he would move about with the instrument in a scooping movement, as though chasing away, or gathering, insects.

I found the piano part perfectly possible, so we played these pieces with pleasure. I had time during the clarinet's flourishes and outbursts to find the right notes, and in any case Maurice was too busy scooping insects to notice.

'God,' he said, when we had finished, 'what a genius I had then.'

He beamed as he sucked his reed and blew little whistling noises down it. Then on an impulse he put his instrument down and started rummaging among the scores on the piano. When he had found the music he was looking for, he opened it in front of me. It was a trio for clarinet, viola and piano.

'Do you think you could manage that?' he asked me. 'My brother's coming to stay next week-end to look at my viola sonata, and we could have a bash.'

I was both seduced and alarmed. His brother was Hugh Arne, of the Con Amore String Quartet. Maurice's playing of his clarinet had sounded to me as cheerfully hit-or-miss as his piano had been, but he could do what he liked because he had written it and presumably knew it backwards anyway. My sight-reading skills were minimal, and Hugh was a professional.

I turned the pages, like a platoon commander surveying terrain to be occupied by his wounded and demoralised men, identifying the banks of semi-quavers like machine-gun emplacements, the concealed minefields of key-changes, and some alarming ambushes of accidentals.

'Wonderful,' I said. 'I'll give it a go.'

8. Trio

I had managed to have the NAAFI piano tuned and moved to the Education Section Music Room. I don't think it was missed, since tannoy music was preferred. There were even newer songs coming out of the tannoy now, aggressive, rhythmic, lewd, that simply could not be ignored. After hearing 'Don't step on my blue suede shoes', what self-respecting airman was going to suggest a sing-song round the piano? The few real musicians on the station, such as the saxophonist who could squirt out whole solos of Lester Young, hitting about 70% of the notes, had found other, more serious places to play, such as the pub in Gloucester that had jazz evenings in an upstairs room. I sometimes went there, in the small general company that liked such things, after a blow-out at the only Gloucester eating-place friendly to us, the proprietor proud of serving us his large pork steaks. On such evenings I wished that I had the skill to improvise. I wished that I played any of the wind instruments that had been annexed by jazz. In deafening proximity to the random assortment of players who congregated in that upstairs room I could see how jazz worked (or sometimes didn't work) far better than in my recordings (West Coast for preference, very bizarrely-scored and laid-back).

I was used, too, to seeing how music worked in theory, from the staves, but only in piano music, and after I had taken it to the keyboard. I found it too difficult to hear music from the page alone. With Arne's Trio I really had to spend most of my time getting to grips with the piano part. I could find those elements in the clarinet's line that suggested an argument or accompaniment from what I was doing below (or sometimes above) it, but the viola's part remained a mystery, being written in a strange clef.

The first movement required eight quavers to the bar of relatively simple support from the piano to begin with, but an increase in tempo brought surges of angry semiquavers and bass chords that taxed my bitty technique. The slow movement was nearly all spread chords of a somewhat glutinous character, and the last movement required a thin texture of single staccato notes drawn from wildly different areas of the piano. The busy-ness of the instrumental lines in this movement suggested that it might not matter if I hit a few wrong notes. I wasn't even sure upon what principle the right notes *were* the right notes. But before the movement came to a close, those surges from the first movement returned, and (help!) the piano now seemed to have much more to do, including the tune, in high octaves.

I took a deep breath and returned to Charlwood the following week-end. After a chaotic launch into the first movement, in which Maurice, of all people, missed his entry, and I played only one hand for at least two pages, I asked if we could try the second movement. I'm sure that Maurice was sensitive to my incompetence since he readily agreed. I'd practised this movement much more, since the notes of the piano's rich chords needed to be identified, but the tempo allowed me just enough time to find them afresh. I even had time to look at Maurice and his brother as they wove their tranquil interlocutions together, nudged and propelled by the statements of the piano. When playing quieter passages, Maurice pulled a sort of clown's mouth and closed his eyes with delicately-lifted eyebrows. He might have been a glass-blower. His brother Hugh, on the other hand, was extremely matter-of-fact, looking up occasionally at Maurice as he might have looked up at the kitchen clock, to make sure that he wasn't over-boiling an egg. His viola seemed rather large to me, not just tucked under his chin as a violin would be but supporting his whole head. It was like a game, where you had to stop the head rolling off, an effect made all the more amusing by the solemnity of the head and the darting movement of the eyes.

I was able to observe all this more freely when they went on to the serious business of the day, Hugh's playing over to his brother of the new viola sonata. Paula brought in a tray of tea (Margaret was visiting friends) and sat down to listen. But it was very noticeable that Hugh's boy-friend Dan, a sour dwarfish painter, dressed rather unusually in a black leather motorcyclist's jacket, went on reading the newspaper and took no interest at all in any of Maurice's music. It might have been the radio in the background, with the Test Match, for all he seemed to care.

I was now considered off-duty, and perhaps required to listen to Paula's small talk with Dan. But it was that special category of small talk that presumes to a large degree on family issues and movements and allows few points of entry to a stranger. Dan's own responses to her questions took the form of regrets, complaints, anger at misunderstandings, frustration at missed opportunities, boredom with fools, and other general dissatisfactions with life. Suddenly, far from seeming permanently withdrawn from the company, wishing he had not come, walking in the garden thinking lofty thoughts, or with his nose in the newspaper, he was voluble, gossipy, launching into interminable whining anecdotes. Paula wore the glazed questioning smile of practised sympathy. When she asked about Hugh's affairs, he would give a little sigh of dismissal.

'Oh, everything goes swimmingly for Hugh, as usual. They're practically resident on the Third Programme, the quartet.'

I tried to discover what sort of thing he painted. For a few years now it had become fashionable to paint cluttered breakfast tables, with cornflake packets, rather than tortured hedgerows vaguely suggestive of crucifixions. The spiritual pain of wartime had been succeeded by a down-to-earth democratic optimism. From what I gathered, it was more likely to be cornflakes than crucifixions with Dan, but he wasn't very responsive to my questions. In fact, he didn't show any interest in me at all, which quite surprised me as I was fairly used to homosexuals being flirtatious. Oddly enough, I met him again about three years later, in the French Pub in Soho. It was typical of him that he showed no sign on that occasion of ever having met me before, but was in a different mood altogether, shrieking with laughter, and quite drunk.

Paula was being nice to him for Hugh's sake, I thought. But apart from having brought him to Charlwood in the first place, with little more purpose, I imagine, than to lay claim to the right to do so, Hugh ignored him for most of the time. He was simply established as an appendage, and possibly only recently established at that, so perhaps he was still being shown off.

Hugh was quite unlike his brother in all respects except something about the eyes and nose. There was a shrewdness and a gleam there, but it was all very much under control. His manner was brief and dry, unsmiling even when something like a pleasantry passed his lips, and those eyes stared out at you, taking everything in and giving very little back.

His playing seemed to me rich and controlled, nothing overstated, but not much passion, either. With that great instrument wedged in his neck, it appeared that his body was effectively cut off from his playing. The bowing and stopping was graceful and accurate, but like a mechanism set in motion: only the head was truly alive, only that severed head with its observant eyes was in command.

'Have you sorted out the bowing, darling?' asked Paula, when Maurice came over to feel the teapot, and Hugh was putting away his instrument.

'That's the least of it,' he muttered. 'I rather think that Hugh would like to rewrite the whole movement.'

Paula couldn't resist launching into a friendly remonstration.

'Oh, Hugh!' she said, as he too came over to join us.

But she couldn't bring herself to say any more. Hugh's interruptive eyes had seemed to precede him, and somehow to forbid any facile rebuke. When he sat down it was with an air of established impregnability. She turned her exclamation into a kind of greeting by immediately going off to get more hot water. I rather wondered why Mrs B. wasn't there to do it.

In her absence, Hugh put his hand out across the sofa and rested it on Dan's knee. He looked briefly at him, without evident warmth, but with enough attention to establish a contact, to convey his concern. It was as if to say: 'Bear up, we'll be away from here soon.' I was shocked by this. I didn't think that Maurice had particularly noticed it, and perhaps it was designed not to be seen by him. I was shocked not so much by the physical gesture and its evocation of an unimaginable sexual contact, as by its accompanying disloyalty, or the sense of an unswerving choice between conflicting loyalties. I had a vision at that moment of the perfectly functioning musical career ditched like a shot at the selfish demand of a dirty Bohemian painter, who couldn't finish his canvases in time for a promised exhibition or who expected his debts to be indefinitely postponed.

'Hugh is my Censor,' Maurice was saying. 'He's always known the difference between the music I should be writing and the music I think I can get away with. Isn't that so, Hugh?'

'If you say so.'

'It was Hugh who suggested the trio, for example. "Why don't you write a trio using the Kegelstatt instruments," he said. Didn't you, Hugh? Said you were fed up with playing string trios. You know the Mozart Clarinet Trio, don't you, Johnny?'

Indeed, I did. I had listened to it on a blue-leather wind-up gramophone that had followed us about during my father's postings in the war. It was among the first music that I ever heard, and I got to know it well. I said something of this, and Hugh turned his piercing blue eyes on me. I guessed that he'd found something outlandish or pretentious in my response.

'So you will be able to tell us, won't you,' he said, sounding more like Mr Parker, my French teacher, than I have ever heard anyone sound before or since, 'whether Maurice has profited from Mozart's example?' His lips came together twice in a little tic, as though he were kissing the air.

He's playing the martinet, I thought. Did he resent my presence there? Was he jealous of Maurice's friendship with me? And what on earth could I summon up to say about the magnificent Kegelstatt Trio? I saw a safe way out.

'One thing's for certain,' I said, with an assertiveness that made even the sulking Dan look up. 'Maurice's Trio isn't a bit neo-classical.'

'Bravo, Johnny!' exclaimed Maurice, delighted. 'There you are, Hugh. I refuse to don the powdered wig.'

'The powdered *what*?' asked Dan, in disgust. He clearly didn't understand what we were talking about, and was waiting for Paula to return so that he could continue complaining, or waiting perhaps for the moment when they could decently leave.

Hugh sniffed.

'I doubt that Wolfie wore his wig to the skittle-alley,' he said. 'Which was where he wrote the Trio.'

'Supposedly,' said Maurice.

'Supposedly,' agreed Hugh. 'But his music belongs to the people, I think you'll find. It doesn't give itself airs.'

That was enough talk for Hugh. He turned to give his attention to some cake that Paula had brought and accepted another cup of tea. I suddenly saw something shy and boyish in him, an echo of the sort of person he was maybe twenty-five years earlier, when it might have been painful to say anything at all, making him seem stiff and assertive. Did that make me sympathise with him more? I don't think so. He would have been just the sort of earnest contemporary I usually run a mile from, too demanding by half. Whereas Maurice had always been, surely, and would always be, great fun.

It wasn't perhaps wholly true that the Trio wasn't neo-classical. What I might have said to the schoolmasterly Hugh, if I had been given time to think, was that Maurice's naturally somewhat rhapsodic style had obviously been tempered by its negotiations with these instruments, in this particular combination, and their timbre of mutually involved statement and reflection. It was more inward looking than anything else of his that I had heard. The eloquence of the clarinet is not, in any case, so much an eloquence of expressiveness as of equilibrium. Whereas an instrument like a violin can always seem to be on the verge of savagely tearing things apart (a supremely romantic solo instrument) the clarinet's best effect is of seamlessly sewing them up.

I thought this true as well of my favourite jazz clarinettists, such as Johnny Dodds. The great blasts of wild trumpet in Dixieland jazz, so necessary to the raw energy of the music, also required the patient and translucent arpeggios of the clarinet, which buttoned up again whatever had been torn. The dialogue of clarinet and viola shared this sort of creative partnership, in Maurice's reading of the instruments. It was an instinctive balance and sharing of the musical ideas, and inevitably carried some of the pacifying gravity of the Kegelstatt.

There was no possibility of my coming up with observations of this sort in the Arne living room. I wasn't quick-witted enough. And there were other things that began to occur to me that I didn't think I would ever be able to say, such as that it was absurd for Hugh to play the viola and Maurice the clarinet. It should, from the point of view of temperament, have been the other way round. Perhaps they were mysteriously switched in youth. Perhaps they each simply developed into the opposite of his instrument, showing up some past stubbornness or misguided parental choice.

Later, I heard of their older sister Fiona, who by all accounts was a brilliant pianist, but had married a farming cousin and lived an isolated and bracing life in the Orkneys. I never met her, but imagined her as the missing element of the real-life trio, and an organising influence, mediating between the different characters of her younger brothers as Mozart's piano does between the other voices of his Trio. A photograph of her that Maurice showed me revealed a bold, severe face, the hair plaited and pinned up, the whole effect rather old-fashioned, as though hearkening back to a different generation. Perhaps it was the Mackenzie in her, and in Hugh. Perhaps Maurice had taken after the other side of the family, more impulsive, more volatile, and had assumed full licence to play the tearaway youngest child.

And yet, of course, the young tearaway, who had continued to tear his way through school and through the Academy, notably precocious as a composer, had at some point become a husband and father. It was the quiet brother who had chosen the unorthodox private life, largely solitary, or only uncertainly partnered, while the tearaway had chosen to play a new role (literally, like a different instrument) in the primary human trio of the family.

I thought of Maurice, Paula and Margaret, too, as representatives of this trio, each required to contribute their own distinctive sound to the ensemble, adjusting it to the demands of the other instruments. But what did Maurice now play in this new combination? How had it affected his music? It amused me to play with the possibilities in those drifting speculations that occur before sleep. I decided that if he was in fact still in command of the clarinet, then Paula and Margaret were a pair of French horns, roundly assertive, but limited in range. The music produced was as banal in tone colour as a harmonium, but that didn't mean that it wasn't worth listening to.

9. Lessons

Parents always look like impostors. I knew well from the surprises at school on our prize-day and other public occasions, when those utterly strange human beings who had created my friends were at long last shyly acknowledged (or insufficiently concealed). I knew that even my own parents, so dearly loved, brought with them the aura of a world different from the one that at school I had been compelled to create for myself. I belonged to them in general, but here they belonged to me, and my own friends would look at them as though in some way it was I who was responsible for them and not the other way around. The growing child is in the process of exploring his own uniqueness, and I certainly thought my own friends were unique to the point of Dickensian grotesqueness. How very strange it was to suddenly be given on these public occasions (when parents were allowed to invade the sacred spaces they had chosen for their children to inhabit) the long-awaited opportunity to study the twin sources of the genetic mix! These parents, they always looked like the guesses of a genealogical cartoonist, crude approximations of distinctive features that had accidentally come together in the faces of my contemporaries. And it wasn't only the biology. Even in their suits, and hats, and dresses, and in their exaggerated politeness to the young, they were unnerving. I could never quite believe in any of them.

Despite Margaret's Mauriceish look, I could imagine Paula having given birth to her, since they evidently came out of the same mould. It was one redolent of health, plumpness, straight hair and downiness, a reliable product, like a seasonal vegetable. Whatever appetite for life they shared was equally moderated or contained. They accepted the roles that life had allotted them, which was to develop and maintain the optimum shape and contour for containing their temperate blood and the organs of their bodies, compact, blonde, muscular and perfectly nourished.

But how was it, then, that Maurice's features spoke from her daughter's face so clearly? As always, I found it fascinating to observe the alchemy of parenthood from close quarters. Not least puzzling is the suggestion of sexual rivalry in the mix: the brutal father imposing a jaw-line, the cunning mother insinuating a dimple. It was hard to imagine Maurice fathering a child at all, since his energies were musical and mental and his physical presence angular and gauche. To think of him begetting Margaret in an intensity of male passion was like trying to visualise the carnality of a humming-bird. She should have inherited gestures and grimaces that only belonged to his imagination, not the line of a nose or a distance between the eyes.

I thought that the occasion of such a begetting must make of a man a great hero in the story of his bodily life. Till then the sexual role has been merely a theory, a wild dream or an affliction.

And it is over in a moment! Supposing that it wasn't? Suppose that it was the sexual act itself that took nine months, and the birth a shudder of a few seconds? The sharing of time between the different functions of pleasure and pain would have more justice, I supposed, but the human race would have long since starved to death. Back to the affliction, the beautiful triviality of orgasm, the isolation of its function, the waste.

But what would a man do when his real productive moment was over? Would he try to repeat it? Evidently not, in Maurice's case. As an only child myself, I had no reason to question Margaret's uniqueness, and therefore I had no reason to wonder why Maurice and Paula had no more children. If they seemed ever so slightly offhand with Margaret, it didn't mean that they disliked children. It might well mean that they liked them very much, so much in fact that they could be treated familiarly as adults. Certainly, they treated Margaret with distinctly more respect than the Pig. But there you are. The child is a symbol of passion, whatever else it may become. It will always embody that unpredictable coming together. It will have no instinctive understanding of that coming together itself, of course, perhaps no conscious acknowledgement of the unbelievable sexual encounter. The child will have its own path to follow, which always has to be a divergence.

But in the case of an only child, the missing brothers or sisters are ghosts who can return to haunt you at any moment. And why do we say an 'only' child, with its unavoidable overtone of 'only a child'? It's as though it is simply the token possession of the wary couple that must remain forever a child to remind them of the amazing effrontery of ever having had one at all. As though it must stand in for all ghosts, sign away independence and become that third necessary element of the triangle, a child only?

Far from repeating the productive moment, or even needing to preserve it for ever, Maurice was now proposing to send his daughter away to the most notorious school in the country, where 'advanced' had ceased to have much to do with educational theory and had simply become an indication of the expected emotional precocity of its pupils. This was cutting the cord with a vengeance. But I supposed that it was easier for fathers than for mothers to do it.

Anyway, I didn't really think that about the school. I'm sure that I was just jealous of those who had been cheerfully sent there, since my own single-sex school had had something very obvious lacking.

Maurice didn't want to send her on her way ill-equipped for the academic life that undoubtedly would never be provided for her there but asked me if I would teach her some modern languages. He made it sound as though any indeterminate amount of such a commodity might be quite useful, like cooking or sewing. He didn't specify which languages, or to what standard, of for what purpose. I think that there was no purpose, since Margaret was decidedly booked for an appearance in the next autumn term, and could, as I understood it, opt for whatever subjects she liked, or opt for no subjects at all. But Maurice must have had some distant memory of the trials of Common Entrance or have felt that Margaret needed to be brought up to scratch. I could do French, couldn't I? What about some German? My O Level German had just about coped with half a page of translation for our Station journal (called *Flight*, rather like a very hole-in-the-corner poetry magazine) but I really didn't think that I could pass on any of my ill-sorted information about that language to Margaret. French, perhaps. I imagined reciting Éluard to her, and introducing, in the guise of grammatical explanations, some of the notions of surrealism:

Le poisson avance
Comme un doigt dans un gant.

'Like a what?' asked Margaret when she heard my explanation at our first session. 'Why should a fish swim into a glove?'

I should have known that explanations were useless.

'It's poetry,' I said. 'It's an idea.'

'I should have thought that ideas ought to be true.'

'Not always. Anyway, it depends what you mean by true. If you want truth of a certain kind, an absolute sort of truth, you'd have to think in mathematics like Bertrand Russell.'

'Ugh,' said Margaret.

'Exactly,' I replied. 'We're not Bertrand Russell, so we have to think in language, which is full of ideas which aren't particularly true.'

When Margaret was puzzled, she pressed her lips so hard together that they disappeared, leaving a rueful fissure above the jut of her chin. Her pained sadness made me want to laugh.

'Look, why is a foxglove called a foxglove? Why is your pony called Danger? You don't think he's dangerous? You don't *want* him to be a danger? Foxes don't wear gloves, do they?'

'I should jolly well think not.'

'Well then, why shouldn't a fish jolly well swim into a glove?

You could think of the darkness of the inside of the glove as being like the immensity of the ocean.'

I was quite pleased with this explanation, but, as always, not sure how to deal with Margaret. I had only just managed to stop myself from embarking on a fantasy of dapper foxes pulling on yellow kid gloves, which might have amused a six-year old, but not someone who was old enough to pretend to have heard of Bertrand Russell. The next thing she said stopped me in my tracks.

'Anyway,' she said. 'Anyway: I don't see why it can't just mean "like the finger of a glove." Can't it? Can't it?'

She was interpreting my pause as defeat, and continued decisively:

'Yes, you see? Gloves have all sorts of things, fingers, thumbs, buttons to do them up with at the wrist. The fish swims like the *finger* in a glove. It's like a pointy finger, that's all!'

She started to jump up and down in front of me, in glee that she had stolen from me the immensity of the ocean. Then she stared into my eyes in solemn triumph, her freckled nose not more than an inch from mine.

'What's the French for wrist? Don't you know? Why don't you know? What's the French for foxglove? You don't know that either, do you? You're useless!'

These friendly attacks became a common feature of what Margaret ceremoniously called 'lessons.' It pleased her to have discovered my uselessness, but she kept it a secret, since she seemed equally pleased by the lessons, and by the opportunity that they gave her to wield her power over me. From staring me out she progressed to hand locks and climbing on my knees, always with the excuse of some argument about her French translation. Once she defiantly licked my nose, but I took this to be some form of disgusting punishment rather than an erotic invitation.

Was it given as such? I was young enough myself to be quite open about such fine distinctions, and too inexperienced in general to be embarrassed, or curious about the implications. I thought that to be licked on the nose was a fine thing in itself, actually, indicating a pleasantly relaxed social relationship. At times Margaret didn't seem very different from a restless puppy.

At the same time, I was disturbed as well as fascinated, knowing that if either of her parents had chanced to come into the room the French lessons would have been exposed as the sham they really were. I tried to interest her in Maupassant's story 'La Parure', which I had studied at school, but her grasp of the language was too uncertain to keep her on track. Teaching was an utter mystery to me. I seemed to have neither the time nor the power to establish a definite programme of work, or to create a pedagogic character for myself. I thought of being Mr Parker, but it was too late to establish a sardonic mask of friendly cruelty. She would have seen through it in an instant.

I envied my Oxford friend Michael, who had written to say that he had a vacation job tutoring a boy in Berkhamsted, rising at 6 am to read the *Iliad*. He had earned £7.10 in one and a half weeks. It wasn't the money I envied, though I wasn't sure if I was going to get any from Maurice or if I were just doing him a reciprocal favour. It was in Michael's case the air of a role taken up casually and professionally that impressed me. Michael complained that he had failed to win a University prize, but he was still able to get up at 6 am to prepare his teaching (or perhaps the *Iliad* was his own study, which he was simply getting out of the way). He was looking forward to me (and other friends of ours currently doing National Service) coming up. So was I, but it seemed a very long way off. I planned a visit to Michael at Trinity College to tide me over.

It was during one of Margaret's teasing inquisitions that I discovered that she was quite aware of Maurice's film about her.

'I thought it was supposed to be a secret,' I said.

'How can it be a secret?' she replied. 'How can you possibly make a film about someone in secret?'

I admitted that it certainly sounded improbable.

'He pretends it's just home movies, but I know what's going on. It's not home movies. It's art.'

She said this with a sigh of resignation, but out of politeness she modulated her mock-despondency into a serious question.

'What are your films like, then?'

I despaired of interesting her in my films, least of all the one I was now planning under the influence of *The Petrified Dog*, a documentary about walkers on Blackheath and their sinister self-absorbed manias. I told her about the one I had made partly at school and partly at the Windlesham house of an English master, with the help of his daughter Ann and a school friend called Gavin. Gavin sets off to get help after a road accident but enters a dream world of a total lack of volition, sliding inertly over the ground, flying through a wood, and becoming distracted by Ann in a bed in the middle of a field, untangling a ton of rope. It was pretty much like *Un Chien Andalou*, but without the violence. It had a gracious ending, where Ann receives a large seashell from Gavin, curtseying in a cemetery overgrown with seeding grasses. I didn't know it at the time, but this extemporised scene was probably the best of any in the films I made. The rest of it, often pixilated in the manner of Norman McLaren, was extremely silly.

'I'd rather be in a film like that,' said Margaret decisively. 'Couldn't we make a Three Stooges?'

'Who would be the stooges?'

'Me and Annie and Pet,' said Margaret, promptly. 'Pet would be a hoot.'

'Why don't I know this Pet?'

'Pet is at school. But she'll be home soon, for the holidays. How's about it, pardner?'

This revelation of Margaret as a devotee of the Three Stooges and Westerns amazed me, but of course on reflection I could see that it was entirely natural that Maurice would take her to the cinema. Could I make a slapstick comedy in Gloucestershire in my spare time? I thought I had put filming into cold storage while I was in the RAF, apart from editing and planning. And there was the invitation (which hadn't come to much yet) to work on Maurice's film. So I said something ambivalent, to the effect that no Hollywood star would ever work on two films at once.

'Well,' she said, firmly. 'I could write a script.'

'You do that,' I said. And I felt as insincere as Darryl F. Zanuck.

Maurice's film, insofar as I could understand it at all, was a film about Margaret without Margaret, and a kind of ballet without people. It contained things, of course, particularly Margaret's things, and it contained parts of Margaret. Bits of it, when he showed me what he had got so far, looked rather like Léger's *Ballet Mécanique*. Some of it was suspiciously like Stan Brakhage. There was quite a lot of the pony. And stop-motion animation, which was much more carefully done than mine.

'It will all be in the music, you see,' Maurice explained. 'I want to cut it carefully, in synch, like Disney's Fantasia. Much the best film ballet, don't you think?'

He pronounced the title with a stress on the third, not the second, syllable, which surprised me more than the idea that Disney's film was ballet at all.

'Well, it *is* ballet. Even when he makes a story out of a tone poem or a Beethoven symphony (for goodness sake!) the movement always wants to become dance. And the best ones, like the Tchaikovsky and the Ponchielli, are pure ballet to begin with, and they have all the freedom of the screen, too.'

It was true, and I have since had the opportunity to check it out. Disney's *Dance of the Hours*, for example, with its complacent ostrich Markova, its disproportionate crocodile-and-hippopotamus *pas de deux*, its ecstatic if occasionally flummoxed *corps* of elephants, is at once a hilarious critique of the conventions of classical ballet and a fresh and exhilarating exploitation of them, like the parody of Italian opera in John Gay. The speed of the skating fairies in his Nutcracker Suite or the protozoic growth of the ocean organisms in his *Rite of Spring* goes so far beyond the capabilities of human performers in a theatre as to lift the music to a strangely different, if substantively irrelevant, sphere altogether. The sheer scale of Disney's *Rite* seems in a way entirely more appropriate to the scale of the music than does the original scenario of the ballet. It is the instantaneous freedom of the screen in place and in time that does it.

I gathered that Maurice wanted the same freedom to interpret his music with images that would change character according to his fancy, or rather to Margaret's fancy, since the film was to represent what was going on in her mind.

'It might well turn out to be almost entirely like this,' he said, thoughtfully. 'A sort of cartoon of real objects, illustrating a musical fantasia.'

74

'"Margaret's Fancy"?'

'Oh, yes,' agreed Maurice, eagerly. 'An Elizabethan title. Why not? Giles Farnaby, his Toye, his Dreame, his Reste.'

'"Margaret's Toy"?'

'Too nursery, I think. There will be toys in it, do you see, in any case.'

Maurice looked at me slyly.

'I'm rather interested in the sexuality of toys, as a matter of fact,' he said. 'Did you know that someone is now making dolls with genitals?'

I didn't know.

'Whereas really,' he went on. 'Really and truly, dolls are themselves genital substitutes.'

He looked at me defiantly, but I wasn't in a mood to argue with him. Besides, he was probably right. I brought him back to the matter at hand.

'Is that what *The Nutcracker* is about?'

'*The Nutcracker!*' he shouted. 'By God, yes! Now there's a thought.'

He smacked his fist into his palm, and then gave a faint little laugh, as if the thought was that he might write another *Nutcracker* but knew that he wasn't up to it.

One of my tasks in the film, it soon turned out, was to create a subjective camera-eye sequence of Danger galloping through a nearby spinney, something that he would never of course do, but which would therefore be all the more dreamlike. It was to be achieved by stop-motion. I had done this sort of thing before and could work out the necessary distance between each single frame (twenty-four per second) to produce the speed of a gallop. I decided that I should keep in as straight a line as possible, and if I came to a tree I would just step round it at the last possible moment. That way the pony would appear to be galloping through it. We discussed whether the height of the camera should be at the level of Margaret's eyes or the pony's and decided on a compromise: I would hold the camera on my head, so long as I could keep my finger on the button that released a single frame. This would provide a satisfying consistency of glide and swoop. The rhythm of galloping would be provided by the music.

After a morning of this sort of thing, I would find Maurice in his study, apparently doing nothing at all. He would bounce up and take me through to the kitchen, shouting out to no one in particular: 'Where's our lunch?' and taking the lids off bubbling pans in mock-interrogation. Mrs B. would be there, so he would feel that he had to explain himself:

'We've been working awfully hard, and we're terribly hungry. Aren't we, Johnny?'

I was embarrassed by this, because I imagined that Mrs B., unlikely to distinguish clearly between vocational labour and idle play, would think that I only came to Charlwood to feed myself and loll on the sofa with a gin and tonic. For Maurice's first-person plural was dangerously of the kind used by nurses, carefully excluding himself.

If this was more or less justice in my case, it didn't solve the problem of when Maurice did all his work. He was not to be seen doing it at weekends, nor did he much share in the various tasks he set me. Yet work he did, since there were always the latest results of it to show me. The various public duties that he performed, lectures, committees, commissions and trips to London, came and went without fuss. And he had students, some private, some from the local college, all of whom seemed not unnaturally devoted to him.

These students didn't need very much teaching as far as I could see. They knew exactly what they were up to. They produced scores, written on very large sheets of paper, of highly theoretical music, which Maurice was obliged to read and annotate to prove that he had read them. I saw some of these scores and thought that he was excessively reserved and polite. For all I could tell they were works of genius, but the nature of Maurice's comments ('You are in danger of producing a melody here' or 'B double-flat?? Why not A double-sharp???') showed him in most cases to be bored into facetiousness. And I thought that to bore Maurice must be the worst sin in the world.

10. The Cautious Man

But perhaps it was being bored that was sinful. To live life fully whatever it has to offer is an undeniable virtue. The unignorable boredom of the Innsworth life stirred in me a silent protest as the summer deepened. Uniforms were belted sweat. It was like standing up to the waist in water. The mild pleasures of the day, the coffee swindle, for example, with the free but always limited choice of bridge roll (grated cheese, cucumber, mashed tuna) became sterile and paltry. The rituals of work that pretended to have some military rationale became more irritating. Someone decided that we would now march to work at 7.50 am. The Flight Sergeant roared with laughter:

'Station Head Quarters Orderly Room and Accounts Flight, 'shun!'

Hurried inspection.

'Where's Corporal Black? If I've got to march you to work in the morning, I'm going to see I'm not lonely.'

But Corporal Black had decided that he had never heard of marching to work. Since the smooth running of Accounts, and in particular the daily balancing of the books, depended entirely on his infallible intuition and good will, there was no one, not even the Flight Sergeant, who was going to remind him of marching. And besides, he organised the football.

'Go and arrange football, Sarge?'

'Eh?'

'Down to 5 PDU. Football.'

'And who said you had a sports afternoon, eh?'

'!' (A smile of confidence, bonhomie and fait accompli).

'You go and arrange football and you don't tell us and then you want a sports afternoon.'

Of course, no one could not want a sports afternoon, and sports afternoons seemed to be more freely available in the better weather. I could myself take the opportunity to escape if I wanted to, and visit Charlwood.

I thought that life itself was like a visit. At the moments when we are conscious of it, it is like a place we have longed to visit, vaguely familiar from our expectations, but dissatisfying in its sometimes uninvolving surprises. Even then I was a devotee of the comforting routine, enjoying the uninterrupted play of my own thought better than any treat. But at what point, when the treat looks like being perpetually possible, does one conformity begin to look like another? Suppose every afternoon to be, miraculously, a sports afternoon. Would Corporal Black be keen to escape into some other activity? Would his desire for eccentric leadership be unsatisfied? Conversely, was I looking to Charlwood not for adventure, creativity, romance, but simply as somewhere I could be unassailably, invisibly, soothingly, at home?

That seemed ridiculous, because I was perfectly at home at home. I already had a home, lucky to be able to share all my interests with my father, reasonably adept at fielding the possessiveness of my mother, left to my own devices, given money. I could get there at weekends. Why should I be attracted to Charlwood?

There are places that are such magnets. Everyone knows instinctively that they must be there, at whatever cost to other allegiances or commitments, simply because they know that whatever is going on there shouldn't be missed. Were you to ask them what of importance had actually occurred on any particular afternoon or evening that had been of benefit to them, they would have been gravelled. Why, they would say, I was at Court, or at White's, or at Garsington, or at the World Turned Upside Down, or wherever. What do you expect to 'occur'? Everyone was there as usual. It was wonderful.

I went to Charlwood whenever I could, and it was wonderful.

But it was not home, and it might have turned into a place of adventure. With a shift of gear I might have been an innocent in another kind of novel, about to discover that the Pig worked not for Denzil and Phipps but for the KGB, and that contrary to appearances his greatest concern lay not in crying up the great virtues of a 1946 St. Estèphe but in cultivating local military contacts in the RAF Records Office, or transit camps like Innsworth. But he showed no sinister sign of wanting to cultivate me, nor of interesting me in ten-year old claret either, for that matter, which was not surprising, since my pay after a recent rise was still no more than £3.16.7 a week. Today such a wage wouldn't even cover a bottle of Tesco Vin de Table. It has to be put into a different context entirely when my preferred tipple was NAAFI Double Diamond at 1s/4d (less than 7p). The coach to London was 14/-. I couldn't call myself well off and was glad whenever I could place a poem in a paying magazine.

I had one in the *Journal of Education* in August, which began 'The fur-coated bear, the affable walrus and the bird-like seal' which I made the mistake of showing (in my pride) to Maurice. We were in the kitchen, replenishing the tray of drinks.

'Is this *me*?' he exclaimed, in mock outrage and glee.

I stumbled through my usual explanation of how poems bore no relation at all to real life.

'Really, Johnny, you're such a formalist,' he laughed. 'Zhdanov would have you shot at dawn. You make Shostakovitch look like a party hack. Even Shostakovitch would have you shot at dawn.'

He lifted the magazine away from my attempted grasp, reading over the poem in delight.

'The affable walrus!'

I grimaced at him in apology, not even sure that I had had him in mind at all when I had written it.

'Paula, look!' he exclaimed, when she came into the room, looking for a gin. 'I'm an affable walrus. Am I truly affable? Am I truly a walrus?'

He capered around the room, muttering the poem:

"'Heavy with cold, the arctic seas and fathers of little girls
Are carelessly assuming now their special droves and moods,
And cunningly each cuddly or gruff mask hides the real man,
The denizen more representative..."

Aha, I'm more than a walrus, I'm a representative denizen! Oh, I'm cuddly, I'm very cuddly! And I can be gruff, too, like a billy-goat. You haven't got a billy-goat in your poem, have you?'

Paula lifted her eyebrows at me, and I shrugged.

'I don't think he's ever been quite so silly,' she said, 'as he's been since you started coming here.'

I began to make some sort of apology.

'No, no,' she said. 'It does him a lot of good. Better for him than all of those dull students of his.' And she quickly stroked my back in that encouraging way that wasn't quite sure if it wanted to be a hug or just wanted me out of the way so that she could find the tonic.

Maurice had come over from the window through which he had been orating to the hollyhocks and gave me back my *Journal of Education*.

'What's that about my dull students? What a calumny', he said. 'But it's true, alas.'

He cut himself a piece of bread, breaking and twisting the crust like a wire puzzle, and nibbling it from the inside.

'They have to be told what to do, you see.'

'Isn't that the point of being a student?' asked Paula.

'Not at all,' he replied. 'You know that perfectly well, old thing. A real student must be self-propelled.'

'Like a pencil?'

'Not like a pencil,' laughed Maurice. 'Well, yes, perhaps like a pencil.' He thought for a moment. 'Yes, indeed: the model student is like a pencil! Well done, Paula! The student's motivation and sense of direction is like the lead in the pencil. All the teacher has to do is to sharpen it. The act of sharpening it exposes the next bit of the lead, which until then is hidden in the wood. Rather neat, I think. Like your gin, Paula.'

He took, tilted and sniffed at her glass.

'It's the tooth,' she said. 'It helps. Besides, I couldn't find the tonic.'

'It's here, old thing, it's here,' said Maurice, holding up the bottle. 'Johnny, did you know? My wife has an inebriate tooth. The tooth, the whole tooth, and nothing but the tooth.'

'It's not funny,' said Paula.

'Of course not,' said Maurice, soothingly. 'Does it mean that you're not coming to the river?'

'Probably not,' she said.

'Lovely Denis is coming,' he said.

'Then certainly not,' said Paula.

Maurice laughed.

'You've met lovely Denis, haven't you, Johnny? In terms of pencil, you sharpen him and the lead falls out. So sad. You twist him away in the sharpener and you never get anything more than empty socket at the end. Self-propelling might be better.'

'I wish my tooth was an empty socket, I must say,' said Paula.

'You'll have to have it out, darling,' said Maurice.

'It's a wisdom, remember? I'll have to have them all out.'

'All out, then,' said Maurice. 'Let your teeth go on strike.'

'Cruel man.'

'Are we collecting Margaret from the Caigers?'

'They were going to bring her back after tea.'

'What about her French lesson?'

'I think she was going to give it a miss this week.'

'Oh, Johnny,' said Maurice. 'Do you mind?'

I bowed graciously.

'But we'll go to the river when the pencils arrive, and scribble a bit, won't we? And take some sandwiches.'

'Not if you eat all the bread.'

'I won't, I won't.'

'And not unless you make them yourself. Mrs B. is visiting her sister in Stroud.'

'I knew that very fact! Wouldn't you like to make them?'

'Certainly not. Particularly if I'm not going to be eating them myself. I'm going to take my drink back to bed with the paper.'

'What's the Pig up to?'

'The Pig has some escapade of his own, I think.'

'Well, well,' said Maurice, turning to me. 'It looks as though we are in charge of our picnic arrangements. Goody! We can make our own Dagwood sandwiches.'

He was referring to the sandwiches made by Dagwood Bumstead in the 'Blondie' comic strip: towering interleaved affairs, consisting of unlikely combinations from a determinedly-raided fridge. Slices of mortadella, floppy squares of cheese, iceberg lettuce, ketchup, radishes, cold chicken, mayonnaise, mezzanine layers of bread, more lettuce, ham. I was surprised that he knew of Dagwood. Five years earlier I had been a great, and guilty, aficionado of American comics. Whatever I knew of American culture was only the icing on a great layer-cake of comic-book lore, from the Katzenjammer Kids, through Lil' Abner and Orphan Annie, to Dick Tracy, Donald Duck and war comics (where bayoneted Japanese soldiers would rot in the jungle until they were mysteriously resurrected as dripping vengeful monsters). I thought I had been rightly weaned from such things, and here was Maurice Arne knowing as much about them as all the other things he knew about, like the films of Maya Deren, or the symphonies of Shostakovitch, which I was discovering for myself. In some ways it was reassuring to me. In other ways it was frustrating. I had to tell myself that we were on the same wavelength, but that he had a twenty-year head start at least. Perhaps this was what being a pencil-sharpener meant.

Such banter between Maurice and Paula was as close as they ever got in public. It seemed like a performance put on for my benefit and might have been scripted by an imaginative brother and sister who had only a theoretical intuition of what marital intimacy was like. Or so I thought. Away from each other, their manner was utterly different. Maurice seemed less on show, and readier with his real thoughts. Paula was happier and more self-confident, barking out commands and jokes. In fact, with her the sisterly manner seemed so much more natural and intimate with the Pig, that she might have been more appropriately married to him than to Maurice. No wonder Jack referred to the Charlwood ménage as 'the Dudleys.' There were roles that Maurice and Paula were playing that seemed deeper than husband-and-wife, and I couldn't quite put my finger on it.

Toothache or not, Paula wasn't a Dagwood sandwich person. I suspected her of intending to lunch with some neighbourhood title or hunt widow, or perhaps in hope of a girlish expedition with Margaret when she had been picked up from the Caigers.

She left us to make our approximations of Dagwood sandwiches, holding her gin before her like a medicine.

My sense of these summer occasions has blurred. We were often at the river, sometimes with sandwiches, sometimes with wine, sometimes with Maurice's students, sometimes with just the family. But whatever was going on, Maurice was in his element. He didn't simply lie on the grass. He interwove himself with it, sucked it, wore it in his hair. If there happened to be a rug, he would somehow contrive to get beneath it, rising to make a particular vehement point in his argument, wearing it like a toga. If there was wine, he would get decidedly tipsy, and the overgrown riverside meadow would become his stage, where to an audience of quietly croaking mallards he liked to enact surrealist versions of the newspaper headlines of the day.

I remember a long scene in which the visiting Bulganin and Khrushchev are shown one of the new self-service shops and are induced to buy some premium bonds. In both cases, it was Maurice's fancy that the puzzled commissars believe these novel facilities are pretending (with no chances of success whatsoever) to be non-capitalist enterprises specially designed to fool the Russians. They grin inanely, but are deeply suspicious. Maurice played all the parts, including a fawning but inebriated Anthony Eden, sporting a dock-leaf moustache.

He was also very good as Buster Crabb, caught spying on the fascinatingly secret propeller of the Soviet cruiser, the

Ordzhonikidze, a performance conducted in the river itself, entirely in dumb show. Did Maurice not take off his clothes to swim, or had he in fact fallen in on the occasion that I remember? There was much business of him emerging from the water still wearing his straw hat, which he took off, politely, in Buster Keaton solemnity. The whole donnée was, of course, that Buster Keaton had been mistaken for Buster Crabb and had to improvise his quite inadequate frogman skills at the behest of MI5.

Despite his genius for such sketches, Maurice wasn't politically committed. He was politically knowledgeable, of course, but he seemed to find public affairs more amusing than anything else.

'Politics! Ah, yes,' he would say, settling his head back on his arms, with one ankle on the other knee. 'That difficult art of creating the complicated spaces in which we will finally have nothing at all to do but simply exist.'

'And isn't that a perpetual struggle?' somebody (usually the lovely but earnest Denis) would say.

'Perpetual? Yes, absolutely endless. But what is one to *do*?'

'Indeed, what is one to do, magister?' would be the Denis reply. 'One can't do nothing, surely?'

'Well, Denis, I have the idea that by practising the art of simply existing we may for a time postpone these, shall we say, contextual difficulties.'

'Mustn't we at least be prepared to do something?'

'Ah, Denis, always the cautious man, forever thoughtful of the future. My God, I bet you were a Boy Scout. *Were* you? Were you always prepared? With a big smile and a penknife?'

After a pause, and a shifting of a long grass from one side of the mouth to the other:

'The trouble is that these days penknives turn out to be H-bombs.'

'Shouldn't we be prepared for tyranny in any form, magister?'

'Yes, yes, particularly in the form of the musical establishment and the film industry. Oh, and the Inland Revenue. I mean, Denis, my dear dormouse, what is a chap like me to do? It's all right for Paula, who can run off and be a JP without turning a hair. I don't think I even understand the real world enough to want to live in it. Neither does Johnny. Do you, Johnny?'

'Not really,' I said. 'But I have to at the moment.'

'Of course you do. It's your profession. Penknives and rifles and all that. But you don't mean it. Your mind is elsewhere. Your essential being is elsewhere. By the way, did you ever see that simply wonderful photograph of Shostakovitch in a fireman's helmet? He was purporting to be on air-raid duty on the roof of the Leningrad Conservatoire during the Siege, or at any rate the powers-that-be were purporting that he was there. But where was he really? Where was his essential being? Probably writing that sonata of yours. The photograph was of some sort of impostor. Why else would they have reproduced it on the cover of *Time* magazine?'

'They all ate dogs during the Siege of Leningrad,' said Denis.

'Shouldn't we all be prepared to eat dogs,' said Maurice, 'when actually put to it?'

'Possibly, magister.'

It was at such a moment, with lovely Denis contemplating his unattractive moral duty, or perhaps with other, lazier, less argumentative students simply lolling about toying with vetch or lying supine with two fingers on the base of their wine glass flat to the slowly-breathing stomach, that a strange sight hove into view at the bend in the river.

In the prow of a freely drifting canoe, standing with one foot raised to the rim in the attitude of a conventional statue of a Victorian explorer of the Zambesi, stood a completely naked man. He was staring into the distance, as into impenetrable jungle, oblivious of our party on the riverbank or of anything else.

It was the Pig.

Maurice let out a brief guffaw of delighted disbelief. The canoe floated by, and the Pig, after momentarily turning his head in our direction as though to notice an exotic bird, resumed his distant gaze without recognition. I couldn't imagine what he thought he was up to.

'The Pig lives in a parallel universe, I'm afraid,' said Maurice. 'You wouldn't think that behind the customary business suit there lurked such an intrepid child of nature.'

'Where is he going to?' I asked.

'Lord knows,' said Maurice. 'Chimborazo, Cotopaxi, I expect, or some sort of similar Eldorado:

"The houses, people, traffic seemed
    Thin fading dreams by day,
Chimborazo, Cotopaxi
    They had stolen my soul away!"

The trouble is, he's in danger of reaching the village instead. Did you notice if he had any oars in that boat?'

I hadn't seen any oars.

'I'm quite tempted to let it happen,' said Maurice. 'In fact, I don't see how we can prevent it, really.'

The boat was already out of sight. I imagined it drifting down to Camelot with its nude figurehead. There is something absurd about the unclothed male body that arises from our sanitised expectations of it. We think of it as art, with the eloquent phrasing of marble musculature and the careless comma of a modest penis, but the reality is graceless. The brief revelation of the Pig was of a pallid doughy trunk and blotchy limbs covered in a light sprue of ruddy hair, with a dark red penis lying inertly over its wrinkled purse, like some military trophy still carried symbolically but uselessly into battle, a flag that no longer expects a cheer.

'He will give the Charlwood Sewing Bee something to talk about, I dare say,' said Maurice. 'And nice Constable Hawkins will bring him home again.'

He had settled back in his recumbent posture, the grass having barely left his mouth. It seems to me now, of course, that Maurice's attitude of letting the world pass him by (as he had let the poor Pig pass by) was just the thing to prove his undoing. It wasn't a question of being unconcerned, but of allowing events to take their course as if there were no question of ever influencing them by his actions. Concern was always turned into a joke of some kind.

His concern for Denis, for example, which surprised me by being quite genuine, seemed to be a concern that he shouldn't fall into the musical rut that the heavily-turning wheels of his education were already creating for him.

'The boy is predestined for a Cathedral close,' he would say. 'Denis, the cautious man, the editor of minor Tallis, or perhaps the maestro of a Shropshire Glee Club.'

One of the things that Maurice liked to do was to observe, and to compile, the selected Proverbs of a Cautious Man. As precepts for life, many of them were unexceptionable, as for instance: 'Always take a breath three seconds before you need to' or 'Does this lavatory contain lavatory paper?' Proverbs of this sort were designed to avoid disaster or embarrassment. There were others (such as 'When you have cut your fingernails twice, it will be time to cut your hair') that sounded only doubtfully to be the result of empirical observation, and a quite a few ('Walk in the middle of the pavement and at the sides of your life') that were indubitably more Maurice than Denis. In fact, as I now see, the Proverbs were largely a joke about himself, and hardly proverbs at all, as arising not out of wisdom but timidity. The prescribed musical fate of the lovely Denis was merely a caricatured version of his own, the creative thrust (as he saw it) weighed down by the parochial and the pedagogic. In his natural state, Maurice would probably have never cut his hair at all. It was Paula who made him do it.

Denis was Maurice's stalking-horse when he needed to talk about sex.

'Really, he should be taken in hand. There must be some energetic and public-spirited girl who would do exactly that, some scrubber from the back streets of Gloucester with a heart of gold and infinite patience. What do the lads of Innsworth do when they're at a loose end and bursting with juice?'

I found it hard to disguise my natural bashfulness when Maurice became jocular on this subject, or tried, in however devious a way, to ask me personal questions of this kind. I had my ready formulae, however, and Maurice was probably relieved to accept the impression that such responses gave of a mature objectivity or collectedness about the matter. In truth, the conscript's circumstances were quite naturally accompanied by celibacy, and also by extravagant boasting, and I said as much.

'Quite so,' said Maurice, 'and perfectly appropriate, if I may say so, to a generation just out of school. But Denis is fast becoming a professional virgin in his mid-twenties, and it won't do at all. He needs a grand passion.'

'What does he need it for?' I wondered. 'Surely he doesn't need it to edit Tallis?'

'He needs it to tell him he's alive. You feel it every moment up here when you breathe, and when your heart beats. You've got to feel it down there as well.'

I was surprised at such a little Lawrentian sermon from someone as naturally humorous and reductive as Maurice. It made me think that it was not so much advice as complaint. Was Maurice himself not feeling it 'down there' any more? Had the moment of sexual heroics really passed for ever? Had his own grand passion been ground down by family life?

'Do you know,' asked Maurice, 'what is the most significant Proverb of the Cautious Man, the Master Proverb, the key to happiness and success?'

I asked him to tell me.

'Never ignore the most beautiful woman in any company.'

'It sounds like a recipe for flirting to me.'

'Well, it *is*,' laughed Maurice. 'Of course it is. But it represents a wonderful economy of biological purpose.'

Economy, I wondered? Profligacy was more like it. But at my age it seemed an attractive way to proceed. The only trouble was the unlikelihood of reciprocation, supposing a whole roomful of cautious men, all likely to be ignored themselves. The most beautiful woman in any company (or the only woman in any company, for that matter) surely had much the best of it. I thought of Debbie, one of only two women LACs in the Orderly Room, who sometimes took the White City coach and once, as the great wheeled Leviathan thundered through the darkness, had dozed with her head on my shoulder. I had wondered if at Innsworth she had grown used to not being ignored. I had momentarily fallen asleep myself, with my head against her head. It had seemed a comforting thing to do, but even so I later wondered if she thought I had in some essential way actually been ignoring her.

Maurice wouldn't let it go.

'I'm afraid that it is advice lost on the lovely Denis,' he said. 'You would think he might be interested in Magda, for instance, wouldn't you? Isn't it his great chance?'

I thought myself that anyone would have a good chance with Magda, and that I didn't blame Denis for showing some reserve. Magda put herself on emotional display with all the subtlety of the Pig, except that her exposure was not so unselfconscious.

'Do you have her interests at heart, too?' I dared to ask him.

'If I did, I certainly wouldn't think of bestowing her on Denis,' said Maurice, looking at me sharply. 'And in any case, I don't believe she would touch him if he were the last man on earth.'

I laughed at this.

'I don't think an awful lot of your matchmaking, then.'

'Not matchmaking, dear boy, just idle speculation. To tell you the truth (and you are not to let this get any further, you understand) Magda only falls in love with tall, dark, red-blooded older men—like myself in fact.'

Maurice was looking at me with a very deliberate twinkle in his eye, as if daring me to ask him more, but I didn't. I thought it a ruse to put me off the scent. He knew that I had seen them so often together that I might suspect a liaison, and that to make such a joke of it would defuse my suspicions. Whereas I think I knew very well already that Magda was, generally speaking (and speaking as Corporal Black might speak), randy as hell. I suspected that Maurice was in there with the rest of them, taking his own chances—while allowing these daring confessions to defuse my suspicions. Well, I concluded, let him think he has fooled me, but isn't he really fooling himself?

'Older men': the pleasantry seemed designed to explain why she found me pathetic. In our youth, we are perfectly content with whatever form of confidence we can muster, and if my own was very far from the personal or sexual confidence that by rights youth deserves, it did provide me at least with a detached mental perspective on this lack, and a means of investigating it and exploiting it somehow.

11. On Guard

My friend Mark wrote to me from Cambridge on the eve of some Long Vacation adventure: 'And how are you faring under National Service, the greatest organised waste of man-power since Xerxes had the sea beaten with whips?' I thought this, though evidently true, a little rich coming from him. Somehow (was it an American mother and an American passport?) he considered himself entitled to treat National Service as a condition that only affected other people, a matter of only theoretical sympathy, ready and willing, but essentially uncomprehending, like a male midwife.

Determined not to complain, I played up the comedy. And I created for him a cartoon Charlwood of erotic opportunity. 'Imagine me ensconced on a five-seater sofa,' I wrote, 'while the daughter brings her schoolfriends, one by one, for my inspection.' None of the implications of this was true. There was hardly such a series, and I was the one to be inspected, not the friends. Despite a good deal of whispering and suppressed laughter, the inspection produced little approval or interest except from Margaret's closest friend, Pet Caiger, who might be supposed, from prior briefing, to have heard the most about me.

It was hard to believe that Pet was the same age as Margaret. I mean that as friends and contemporaries they were evidently much the same sort of age, even though I didn't know precisely how old, but the difference was profound. Sexual maturity, like a gift or a charm in a fairy tale, is something that one can unknowingly possess, and its powers can be squandered. Whatever Margaret owned, or had begun to own, was unacknowledged—the swimmer's shoulders, the changing shape of the hips, the glow of down on the cheek, the deepening of the skin as a field of sensation. Beneath these signs her body still moved as unashamedly and as awkwardly as a child's. Pet, on the other hand, though scrawny and without much health or beauty, acted as though a woman inhabited her body and was making quite as much of a bad job as she could. Encountering either of them alone would have been unremarkable, for in either case you would have said that a creature was in transition and that Nature was biding her time. Together, the disproportion was fascinating and challenging.

We are now used to the fashion for exhuming our grandparents' clothes and wearing them in inverted commas. We are used, too, to clothes designed for teenagers. Fifty years ago, it was usual for children to dress as children until it was time to dress as adults. Even children's clothes were obvious versions of what in due time they would find themselves conventionally wearing. Little suits, and dresses with collars and matching cuffs. Short-sleeved dresses with cuffs. At Innsworth dances, if a girl sat on your knee you were aware of the contours and connections of stiff undergarments that would have been recognisable to an Edwardian. Clothes were simply light variations on the appropriate uniform, and more often than not your parents chose them for you.

Pet wasn't like that. She made up ensembles from bits and pieces to suite her moods: a dateless black bombazine blouse with necklace to match, black slacks that her mother might have worn on a Cunard liner in the thirties, and dirty pumps; or, more commonly in hot weather, an ankle-length Mexican print skirt and a white shirt of her brother's, the cuffs undone and hanging beyond the tips of her fingers or sometimes done up and sticking out like short tubes at her wrists, her hands emerging from the slits at the side, below the buttons. This gave her the air of a gypsy waif, or perhaps a marionette representing a gypsy waif, the hands appearing broken or drooping, waiting to be revived by a tug at the strings.

Her eyes were dark buttons, staring at you from beneath unusually hairy eyebrows, the nose thin, the mouth a top-heavy bud in repose that broke into an attractive fierce smile, almost a snarl, whenever she spoke. Margaret introduced us a trifle grudgingly, I thought, as though the encounter could hardly be put off any longer and had to be got out of the way, so that they could go off and—what? Play was hardly the word, I thought, as though their dolls needed their tea, and Pet didn't look like a lover of ponies one bit. So what did they do when they were together?

Pet, however, held out her hand with conscious amusement, looking me full in the face and saying:

'Ah, the tutor!'

I couldn't deny it, exaggerated as such a role sounded, since I didn't want to undermine what little credibility I might still have with Margaret. I was forced to collude in the little charade that Pet was concocting for herself, that of a representative of a county family being formally introduced to a new functionary in a neighbour's household. I merely gave a little laugh, which I thought contained just as much self-deprecation as her own mock-graciousness might want to acknowledge, without actually claiming any other, more significant, identity for myself. I took her hand, which was lightly held with the knuckles uppermost so that it was clearly not meant to be shaken. Not quite knowing what to do with it, I gave it a little lift. The fingers were thin and inky.

'Deeply, very deeply privileged,' said Pet. She held my gaze for a moment longer, and then collapsed against the banisters, weak with laughter. Margaret became slightly irritated—either at the whole performance, or else because Pet's façade had cracked so easily—and dragged her friend away.

It wouldn't have been the first time that I had been left to my own devices at Charlwood. I was a familiar enough presence for almost any member of the family to believe that I was engaged with one of the others. Even if I were found simply reading the newspaper, no one felt it their absolute duty to entertain me.

These were the days when Colonel Nasser had nationalised the Suez Canal Company and Egyptian assets were frozen. I didn't need newspapers to tell me what movements of troops were afoot as a result of this, because I saw it at first hand. Innsworth was a transit camp. Our leaves were frequently cancelled to allow for the extra work involved in getting airmen paid and their affairs sorted out before they were posted to the Mediterranean. I was bored by all this, finding it almost impossible to see the military machine clearly from the outside, and I could hardly be bothered to relate my calculation of Rock Ape allowances to the larger picture of colonial aggression. And of course, there was no one to persuade me to rebel. Even Maurice seemed to believe that the Egyptians were unreliable.

I told him the story of a friend's father who had taught anatomy at the University of Heliopolis in the days of King Farouk. A student had come to his office pleading to be given a passing grade, offering bribes, and when my friend's father refused to be bribed, the student had brought out a gun and shot at him.

'Perfectly understandable,' said Maurice. 'The poor deluded fellow believed that his whole career was at the mercy of a corrupt imperialist power. He would get bad grades simply because he was an Egyptian. He might even have been taught an inferior version of anatomy, reserved for the natives.'

'But some of the students presumably got good grades?' I said, slightly thrown by this interpretation of events.

'Yes,' said Maurice, 'but those would be the students who were able to offer better bribes. What can a poor student do but reach for his revolver?'

'What would you have done?'

'Oh, I would have brought out my own revolver first. Didn't your friend's father carry one? They're absolutely necessary when you're bringing civilization to foreign parts.'

'A strange way to run a medical school.'

'No stranger than the way the whole country is run. I expect the student was a supporter of Neguib, wasn't he? Perhaps he scrounged the grades he wanted and soon was in a position to have some students of his own. Perhaps he was then shot at by one of Nasser's rabble. It's the survival of the quickest, do you see? And if you were going for a brain operation wouldn't you want your surgeon to have triumphantly survived such a process? To be cool in danger? Steady of hand? It would even work with music students. I'd begin by shooting all the admirers of Vaughan Williams.'

I didn't know what to make of remarks like these. Was he not himself an admirer of Vaughan Williams? At least, I had heard him conduct the *Fantasia on a Theme of Thomas Tallis* at Hereford with no less tousled enthusiasm than the other items on the programme, an overture of his own and a Beethoven symphony.

'Not my idea. Not my programme,' he said. 'But never look a gift horse in the mouth. How else will I get performed?'

I was ready to believe that Vaughan Williams was passé, or on the wrong track. He had come to a concert at my school, when we had sung Holst and Howells and, indeed, himself to him. He had been led into the gallery where he sat with his head sunk on his chest, apparently contemplating his waistcoat buttons, much like a bronze bust of himself, already a part of musical history. To me the best parts of his music were not the wandering folk landscapes, but the tortured and rhythmical irruptions, mostly borrowed, as I then believed, from composers like Bartók.

But Maurice wasn't a million miles from the world of Vaughan Williams, or at least, he seemed close enough at times. Did he not consider himself as an 'English' composer?

'You wouldn't think so if I were called... oh, what? Gamal Nasser, or something. Boris Arnovitch, maybe. It's a curse of the name. A double curse, actually, since everybody thinks they've already heard of me: 'Dr. Arne.' Good Lord, I practically wrote the National Anthem, didn't I? Been going strong since the eighteenth century, haven't I? I should have dropped the Arne and called myself 'Maurice Mackenzie', my mother's name. My father's done nothing for me anyway. Though being a Scottish composer is possibly worse because they're all called Hamish McCunt. Still, when you think about it, 'Maurice Mackenzie' has the right sort of alliterative ring to it. Thomas Tallis, Edward Elgar, William Walton, Benjamin Britten... Maurice Mackenzie.

Comforting to the public, do you see? The euphony of the kindergarten. Mickey Mouse, Milly-Molly-Mandy, and so forth. Britten really has it made in all respects, doesn't he? Look at him! His name is also the name of the realm! Bet you he'll be Lord Britten before he's finished, *and* Master of the Queen's Musick. By God, his music *is* the queen's music already, isn't it? Perhaps I should shoot all *his* admirers, too. Last thing I heard he was in Bali writing a comic ballet. Who would have thought it? Willie Walton says that you can't get on at all as a composer unless you're queer. Perhaps it's true.'

When in this sort of mood, well into a third gin, Maurice could go on for ever. At other times he was perfectly prepared to talk constructively about national musical characteristics or about his true likes and dislikes, but his private jealousies always kept bubbling to the surface ('I heard the new fiddle concerto by Rawsthorne last week. Couldn't get my head round it'). I was deeply suspicious of this, especially since Rawsthorne was a composer I much liked (the second Piano Concerto is one of the greatest post-war English works) but I kept my counsel. Maurice was no more snide than most artists who need to look over their shoulder from time to time. I noticed that his best insights into contemporary music were always on offer when he had reason to feel confidence in himself, after listening to a broadcast of his own music, for example. On such occasions he had nothing to be jealous of but oblivion.

'What will happen to us all? Nothing lasts. Think of all the great unrecorded sopranos. Think of the Sumerian notation we have: no one knows what it sounded like! We don't have any of their instruments. They'll invent longer and longer-playing gramophone records and no one will have the machines to play the old ones. Once we start throwing H-bombs at each other no one will have the machines to play the new ones, either. We're doomed. No one likes music any more in any case. Did you know that Elvis Presley is a millionaire? And what did I get for that Dance Suite, including repeats? Twenty guineas. It wouldn't keep Danger in hay.'

Maurice certainly wanted to get rid of that pony. In the film it was to metamorphose and fly away to an unharnessed transcendental existence, as a sort of equine moth, to signal the end of Margaret's childhood. This idea seemed rather a good one to me, if a little fey, but I had no idea what technical means he proposed to achieve it, and I don't think he had either.

I knew what he meant about obsolete machines. We had made a film at school on 9.5mm, already rare then. I have the only copy but have never been able to show it. Perhaps it will never be seen again, even though it exists, like Sumerian music. I thought that Maurice was being a bit melodramatic to suggest that his own work might suffer a similar fate, but he wasn't entirely wrong, of course. The vagaries of taste, sheer forgetfulness, the death of the LP, the physical deterioration of film stock, all these have a part to play. If a copy of *Mission in Moonlight* survives, as I suppose it must, it is the sort of film that is only shown at 9.15 am on BBC2 and half-watched by health freaks on their striding machines.

Is that what all its emotion was for? The concerto, when you concentrated on it without the sentimental visuals, pretended otherwise. As music always does, it commandeered the time you gave to it, drawing you into its sense of fresh experience. And that experience was not only adventure, but mortal risk. I thought of what Maurice had said about music as a language for emotions, and wondered which had really come first, the unknown worldly experience (Jack saying that he wrote it for his student) or its tailoring to the requirements of the screen (Granger's clipped words to Patricia Roc from his blazing cockpit: 'I say, old girl, there's something I'd quite like you to do for me if you would. I don't suppose I'll get the chance now'). This wasn't an unusual question, of course, considering the near-impossibility of putting a personal interpretation on, for example, grand opera. You can imagine Mozart feeling himself into being a rake, or even Wagner understanding what it is like to be a malevolent dwarf, but when music tells the whole story, somehow the personality of the composer has to be subsumed or abstracted. I tried, when thinking along these lines, to imagine Maurice as a puckish, Bohemian version of Stewart Granger, distracted by the Central European refugee girl (played, I think, by Lili Palmer) and only reconciled to his sweetheart (Roc) in the fiery and redemptive dénouement.

Granger of course was playing a pianist-composer in the film, and the refugee pleads to become his pupil, perhaps only to avoid interment, but certainly falling in love with him. That side of Maurice fitted perfectly, but I couldn't imagine him dryly taking to the air and performing diffident heroics. Even at the wheel of his car his conduct was careless and approximate, his signals late and his intentions unclear. He never seemed to change gear and talked all the time. I doubt if he could have driven a Spitfire to the end of a runway.

He was a willing chauffeur, though, and seemed always the one to collect or deliver Margaret to the houses of her friends. He even came to Innsworth on occasion, to save me a rainy wait for the bus. Paula had her own car, which the busy timetable of her own unknown life exclusively required, and it was a much more serious car. I thought it an absurd indulgence for a family to have two cars, and for Maurice to have the ancient drop-head with the stitched hood almost demoralising. But he loved it, and never more so than when it was full of students and he could talk his way between the Gloucestershire hedgerows, stirring the gear handle occasionally if he came to a fork in the road. The ancient seats were made of mummified leather, and the windscreen slanted somehow away from you instead of towards you. There were chrome features of an antiquated kind, and a horn that played the first four notes of the Siegfried motif, an oddly inconclusive phrase that nonetheless wisely invited all oncoming traffic to get out of the way.

The most vivid memory I have of that car is not one in which I was actually in it, strangely enough.

It was during a night of guard duty at camp. Usually I managed to avoid guard duty by paying an obliging and impecunious Scot to do it for me, but on this occasion I had failed to find a substitute. I complained about this with some bitterness since Maurice had offered to take me to a college party.

'Never mind,' he said. 'It's the path of greater virtue. While the emperor and his minions riot, there must always be watchful centurions on the battlements. At least you're at Innsworth, not Wakefield.'

He was referring to the current efforts of the IRA to spring Cathal Goulding from Wakefield Prison. I was always surprised when it was Maurice, rather than my RAF superiors, who reminded me why the camp needed guarding at all. At Innsworth, any mention of the IRA was jocular and mythical, but Maurice seemed to understand more clearly what was going on.

'Goulding's chums will naturally need guns and ammunition,' he would say. 'Pointless to try to smuggle them into the country when they can pick them up over here simply by calling in at RAF Innsworth.'

He made it sound horribly easy, as though the NAAFI list might read: 'Web Equipment Cleaner, RAF, Pickering's Blue/Grey Renovator, 3 oz, tin, 0s 8d; Propert's White, tin, 0s 10d; .303 Rifles, Enfield, £25. 6s. 0d, &c.' and all Goulding's chums would have to do would be to sidle up to the linoleum-covered counter in Stores and put in their order in triplicate, having been unnoticed by the guard on duty who was too busy composing surrealist poems in his head. And Maurice would sometimes make more sinister suggestions. Probably quite soon after I met him, he referred to the nineteen French soldiers blown to bits by the Algerian resistance in the context of my guarding the camp with truncheon and whistle. I think that I was perplexed and affronted, rather than alarmed.

'Surely you're not equating the IRA with the FLN?' I objected.

'Why not?' Maurice beamed. 'The first characteristic of the colonialist mind is not to accept that colonies are colonies at all. The Presbyterian burghers of Belfast are no different from the colons in that respect, and I don't see that Ireland is essentially any different from Cyprus or Egypt. You'd expect to be shot at if you were in those places, I imagine?'

'I don't want to be shot at anywhere.'

'Tough luck,' Maurice sympathised. 'But you presumably decided that you weren't in fact a pacifist?'

I couldn't really agree. I was much against war. But since I was obviously not a conscientious objector, I couldn't disagree, either. I had, regretfully, to be put down with those who had never thought seriously about such things at all. I might easily have been in Cyprus or Kenya or Egypt along with the airmen I had helped to send there, instead of idling my time in Gloucestershire, writing poems and playing the piano music of Shostakovitch (and of Maurice Arne).

I was sorry to miss the party, and nearly as sorry to have actually to endure the guard duty. The first shift was the best. You went on at 5.30 pm, a bare half-hour after work in Accounts came to an end, and finished at 2.30 am. But of course, not only had a whole evening's freedom disappeared, but the following day's routine followed remorselessly. I decided to spend the time on duty trying to remember all that I knew of English literary history from Chaucer onwards (in a series of broad but useful generalisations suitable as a preparation for my reading English at Oxford the following year). The idea was to exploit what otherwise would be a blank and unprofitable period of time in discovering what I knew, and in what form I knew it, and in coming up with novel formulations in the exhilaratingly pure absence of books or notes. What really happened was that I couldn't remember a thing. I couldn't bear to confront my own ignorance, and allowed my mind to wander in triviality and boredom.

A little cat came to my sentry-box at 8 o'clock. It nudged the buckles of my gaiters with its nose and stood proprietorially on my toe cap, with its tail curling round my leg like the tendril of some shooting plant. I recited to it all the cat poems that I knew, but couldn't get very far with any of them:

"'Twas on a lofty vase's side
That China's gayest art had dyed,
Demurest of the tabby kind
The pensive Selima reclined...'

No, I wasn't sure of the order of the third and fourth lines, and besides, hadn't I left something out? The stanza surely ended 'Gazed on the scene below' (like Cressida, or was it Helen, looking down on the returning Trojan heroes, as someone had suggested)? There would have to be another short line earlier, that rhymed

99

with it. Ah yes, the art of China had dyed not simply the vase, but also the decoration of the vase:

"'Twas on a lofty vase's side
That China's gayest art had dyed
  The azure flowers that blow...'

But surely, then, it must be '*Where* China's gayest art...'? I stopped again, and in any case the cat wasn't listening. I tried giving it a piece of chocolate, but it wasn't interested in that either. I think it just wanted to be warm. I put it inside my battledress, where it purred and stirred like a mysterious extra bodily organ. I wondered how anyone could remember poetry without consciously learning it, thousands and thousands of lines, the bard of *Beowulf*, the troubadours, all of them. And how much of English poetry could be retrieved from memory if it disappeared in a world disaster where all books simultaneously crumbled into dust? William Empson could be relied on for most of *Paradise Lost* since he had been able to remember it when evacuated from Peking with his students during the Sino-Japanese War. He also typed out the whole of *Othello* from memory. Actors could get together for lot of other plays. But memory of *The Prelude* would be patchy, and poets like Landor or Herrick largely irretrievable. Hardy's *The Dynasts*, Nashe's *Summer's Last Will and Testament*, Pound's *Cantos*? Lost for ever. Why hadn't I bothered to learn more poetry, since I wrote some myself? I felt lazy and fraudulent and tired.

After I was relieved, I ate a midnight breakfast, one of those ongoing fry-ups that the cooks in C-Section were so good at. When I returned to my sentry-box at 12.30, the cat was still there.

'Why aren't you hunting in the moonlight?' I said to her. I should have remembered to bring her some bacon. She was more alert now, and less affectionate, looking around her as if she could hear things from the hedge across the road. I could hear a car in the distance, louder than the very occasional crescendoing drones that came from the main road. It must have turned off and be coming down the side road. Why? The road didn't really lead anywhere, simply round the perimeter. As it came nearer, my heart leaped. It was an open car, full of gesticulating figures.

I had never seriously prepared myself to confront the chums of Cathal Goulding. To hit even one of them on the skull with my pert truncheon seemed an unlikely folly, and I had already realised that no one in the camp would hear if I blew my whistle. The mild interest that I felt in their political purposes prompted the familiar line from 'The Second Coming': 'The best lack all conviction...' Could I engage them in a conversation about Yeats? I would let them in, of course, perhaps asking them to tie me up, like a timid railway clerk in a Western, the part usually played by the appropriately-named Donald Meek. Or would their 'passionate intensity' take delight in beating me up? Or worse? These wild thoughts took a second or so, and then I realised that the car belonged not to the IRA, but to Maurice Arne.

As it careered past, the occupants waved wildly at me, all except Maurice, who with a manic grin was trying to keep the car out of the ditch, and the lovely Denis, who, in an unlikely display of friendly mock-reverence, turned his head with military smartness in my direction, like a subaltern at a march-past, as if I were an inspecting field-marshal. In my relief that they were not terrorists, I felt immensely good-humoured and warm towards them all, and returned a salute. I presumed that that was it, that someone had said: 'On the way home, go past Innsworth and see if we can see Johnny on guard.' No doubt that was the main spirit of the thing, but instead of disappearing with the same sudden jollity as it had arrived, the car stopped fifty yards down the road, and someone got out.

It was Magda.

'Johnny, Johnny,' she said, as she teetered towards me, a bottle in one hand and a cigarette in the other. 'We have missed you tonight. Look what I have brought you!'

My default position in the sentry box was in theory at-ease, allowing suitable wariness but no distractions. I smiled at her uncertainly, remembering how tourists liked to torment guardsmen in Whitehall. Should I take the bottle? Would she stand there, swaying slightly in front of me, to see how far I would unbend? To my alarm, the car drove off, and with hardly a moment of hesitation Magda stepped into the sentry box with me.

'Johnny,' she murmured, 'you look delicious in your uniform.' She slid a hand inside my battledress, and I thought with amusement of what she would have found there if she had come some hours earlier. There was party wine on her breath, and wine from the opened bottle (now precariously clutched in the same hand that held her cigarette) momentarily dripped on my trousers. She was something like a cat herself, I thought, her narrowed eyes eager and inquisitive as she sought her satisfaction, but at the same time with the glint of the hunter's reserve and cunning. This proximity was a seeking, not an offering. I was sure that she had already decided what to say and to do, and that whatever I did myself would make no difference whatsoever.

Her face had moved out of the moonlight into the darkness of the box; she was too close for me to guess her intentions. Her mouth found my bottom lip and took it in gently between her teeth as though it were the leaf of an artichoke. She gave something like an indrawn sigh, and I dropped my truncheon. Her tongue passed across my lip, and then was suddenly travelling across my cheek, until it found my ear.

Absurdly, I could think of nothing much except what Corporal Black might have said later ('Then I had her in this sentry-box, see…'), claims produced in the section daily, as if by rote, and as frequently disbelieved, claims usually too outrageous to be envied, merely assessed as feats of invention, like jokes or novels. As with so much of life, I was used to standing back from experience, trying to accommodate the general category that it fell into with the irrelevant though unique details that accompanied it. In this case, the distraction of face-powder and onion, the fumes of wine, her unexpected tallness, the strand of her hair caught in my cap-badge, the loudness of her breath, the trespass of her hands, the surprise and suddenness of her entire presence.

Well, I thought, this is at last going to have to lead to something, is it? I was conscious of holding her by the waist like a pot of geraniums, and I wasn't sure that I really liked her tongue in my ear. Whatever else I might have liked didn't seem possible to achieve in the upended coffin we were standing in, but I realised that things had to be taken one at a time. What would I do next?

And then, just as suddenly, it was over. The car hadn't driven away at all. It had simply gone on in order to turn round and go back the way it had come. Magda was not a triumphant gift, like Cressida, delivered at her request. I was not a longed-for tryst, for which she had endured the party. I was a mere paragraph in the larger story of the evening, and Magda the finger that kept the place, for a moment, until the real direction of the narrative, the exciting adventure, had gathered itself and roared off in a new direction. She jumped into the car to licentious cheers. Everyone waved at me, and the car sped away.

I was ashamed of myself for the degree of excitement that I found myself in since I didn't care all that much for Magda. But in sexual situations we are drawn where they lead us. In my case, with her tongue in my ear—for a moment. What did it mean? For someone of her freedom to be in Maurice's circle at all implied that she was, as I had thought all along, in his thrall. But what did Maurice require of her? What did he offer her that she was not content with? I thought of what he had said about pastoral ('He plays his pipe and *thinks* of his shepherdess') and the way that Magda's role in his film was so distant and sad, her fingers intermittently miming the chromatic phrases of the flute on the soundtrack as she danced, quite alone.

I didn't think that the aloneness was of her choosing, or even entirely hers. It was Maurice's aloneness, Maurice as the Sicilian shepherd in the heat of the day piping his purely theoretical and generalised lament. I wondered what the shepherdess's music might have been like. Probably much, much jollier.

She had left me the bottle of wine, at least. It was two-thirds full. Like the soul of an Englishman.

12. Mr. E and Mr. A

Maurice was as inscrutable as ever. He wouldn't say much about the party, not about what had occurred before midnight, nor about what occurred after the group in the car had left me. Since it wasn't even clear to me what had really occurred in between, what its motive was, exactly, or its implications, I was none the wiser for my polite enquiries about the occasion and its purposes. I didn't even know if Magda was enrolled at the college. If not, then her being seen with Maurice (though never, it would seem, at Charlwood) was decisive evidence of an attachment. I already sensed as much, and instinctively never spoke of her there.

But her kisses in the sentry box, were they of her doing alone? Did Maurice know precisely what had happened, or had it fallen simply to anyone in the car to get out while it turned around, and to bring me the bottle of tepid Riesling? Might it have been Jim or Sally, the cheerful pair I had noticed waving from the back? Might it even have been Denis, who knew me best? Or had Magda been earmarked by Maurice, with some tacit understanding, perhaps even an open instruction ('Do be nice to Johnny') that his benevolent authority allowed without it seeming at all crude?

I couldn't imagine what really lay behind such a casual instruction. It was in one sense simply another example of Maurice's friendliness and generosity, like a Sultan's conventional offer to an esteemed guest to make free with his harem. And perhaps I should have felt greatly privileged ('I certainly wouldn't think of bestowing her on Denis') as if singled out among many for special favour. And, like the knowing guest, understand that the offer was merely a convention and not intended to be taken up in fact. Perhaps he considered me with such favour because he knew that I was indeed too civilized to take it up. Too considerate, too reserved, too understanding of his own position. He wouldn't have arranged such a treat for Corporal Black.

Or perhaps I was now to be thought of as in some sense part of the family, or at least part of his household. I was to be trusted with Margaret, and Paula could safely flirt with me (if she wanted to: did she?) so there it was: I was practically a eunuch. It was all very different from the Bohemian morals of Cupid and his friends, or the controlled availability of the WAAFs from the Innsworth typing-pool, or the local nurses.

Maurice's power lay in his insouciant ability to divert attention from whatever was the issue at hand with a joke, or a wry generalisation. Behind the jokes you sensed a real wall of privacy that wasn't to be breached. I would have loved to have known, for example, why he had married someone like Paula, what he was like when he had done so, and how on earth he had managed it. But there was no way into a conversation that might have illuminated any of those riddles. It was, like many other aspects of Maurice's life, left to observation and deduction, which I don't think I was much good at.

Maurice acknowledged the riddle at the heart of creativity. We had been talking about Elgar, and his puzzling motto to the Violin Concerto ('Here is enshrined the soul of...' in Spanish, of all things) usually taken to refer to Alice Stuart-Wortley, with whom Elgar was at the time in love. I think that I confused her in any case with his wife Alice (the 'C.A.E.' of the *Enigma Variations*).

Maurice laughed.

'Alice, Schmalice,' he said. 'Such a uniquely Victorian name, straight out of the nursery. You can take your choice. His wife belonged in the nursery, after all. Did you know that 'E.D.U.' in the *Variations* is her nickname for him? Edoo, little Edward?'

Of course I didn't know.

'God knows what they got up to in the bedroom, little Alice and little Edward. No, no, Johnny. It's none of our business. Anyway, Willie Walton told me that the concerto was inspired by Elgar's affair with an actress who later became K. Clark's cook. They even generated a bastard child, would you believe it? Willie ought to know, I should think. He heard it from Clark's wife, whom he was pleasuring at the time. Does it matter? There's a mystery in everyone's life, so it shouldn't be a surprise to find a mystery in a composer's. But why on earth is one interested? Mr E. the mystery!'

I said something about natural human curiosity.

'Well, of course,' said Maurice. 'But since you haven't actually met Mr E., your interest is unreasonable, isn't it? No, the interest is in the music, and it's the mystery that's in the music. To make the music challengingly fascinating, in relation to the life, I mean, is at once the hardest thing in the world and the most natural. Because of course it happens naturally, and the composer is powerless to do anything about it.'

'So what about the answers?' I asked.

'The answers don't matter,' said Maurice. 'Like the Violin Concerto and *Enigma*, which survives the puzzle, and simply delivers the music, with its emotional charge remaining altogether commanding and mysterious. Is there indeed another theme behind the Theme? People like to think that there is. If there were, what would it tell us? It wouldn't make the music any better.'

'And we don't try to find out?'

'Do what you like. If you want to try to find out, do so. I suspect that finding out is somewhere in your nature. Why are you going to spend three years of your life reading English at Oxford? Is it going to help you to write poems? It certainly won't help you to make films. Perhaps it will turn you into a scholar. The gorge rises.'

I'd stopped being offended by such sallies, because I knew that Maurice hated music critics, and thought that they were all pedants. But given his relish for the Walton gossip, I thought his argument a trifle disingenuous.

'Think of all those dons in carpet slippers trying to find out who Shakespeare was going to bed with,' he went on. 'Is it going to make any difference? I expect the plays simply come from other older plays. Like music. It's all pinched from somewhere else. Look at Willie, for example. Much admired in his infancy for 'Portsmouth Point.' Well, have you heard Honegger's 'Rugby'? No? I suggest you do. That's where it all comes from. And his viola concerto is pure Prokofiev. Anyway, who's your tutor going to be, do you know? I bet he's about ninety and only gets an erection in the proximity of Old High German mutations.'

I said that I thought my tutor would be John Bayley.

'Oh,' said Maurice. 'I know someone who knows him. He's just got married to an existentialist who's written a novel, hasn't he? Practically an Angry Young Woman. Perhaps you'll be all right with him then.'

I said that I thought he had seemed very nice at my interview.

'"Very nice"?' said Maurice. 'You make him sound like a slice of sponge cake. Professor Bayley of Maison Kunz Studies. Don't be fooled. I expect he's got a lot of Old High German up his sleeve. Or the equivalent.'

'I would have thought you might have approved of philology, Maurice,' I said. 'Isn't it like learning harmony?'

'Is it, Johnny, is it?' replied Maurice, trying to show respect, but conveying only a wistful doubt. 'It may be the bones of language, but it isn't the bones of creative language. I don't really know what that might be.'

'Rhetoric, perhaps?'

'Rhetoric?' he laughed. 'Oh dear, you are becoming a perfect pedant after all.'

But I was really interested in rhetoric and knew that I wasn't a pedant. There was a rhetoric of film, too, which I had largely picked up from Eisenstein's books, where he writes about montage and the films of D. W. Griffith and the techniques of Dickens, and it seemed important to me that the relationships between pieces of film, like the relationships between words, could be examined and somehow systematised. How else to explain all the possibilities of contrast, analogy, substitution and spatial dynamics that belonged to the practice of montage? I tried to explain what I meant by rhetoric.

'You know that moment in *The Thirty-Nine Steps* when the landlady discovers the body and turns to the camera to scream, in close-up? You don't hear the scream but only the sound of a train whistle. And then there is a cut to a train entering a tunnel. And then a dissolve to Hannay nodding off in the compartment. That's rhetoric. The invisible point of it all is that she will think that Hannay did it. The murder has been discovered, and Hannay will be pursued. He will know this, but not know when. You see him at a moment when he is least thinking about it.'

'Why rhetoric?'

'Because you have a choice of methods here, and you have to keep the audience informed and interested. The question is, How do you do it? The visual and aural analogies are dramatic. They link the two scenes in a complex way that is both shocking and logical. The scream, the tunnel—a kind of metaphor of fear and pursuit, with the ironical contrast of the landlady's being terrified and Hannay being asleep. The film-maker chooses from his stock of devices just as a poet does, to shape the way he makes the audience see or read.'

'Quite so, Johnny. If you want to call that rhetoric, I can see that you're entirely entitled to do so.'

What I couldn't yet justify was my desire to make films entirely out of such moments, doing away with narrative altogether.

These conversations made me feel for a moment that I should be going to study music or films instead of literature, but I didn't think it was likely that I would take that plunge. I knew nothing about the means for doing so, in any case. And perhaps my tutor, with his new existentialist wife (whom I imagined as being like one of the boulevard café Bacchantes in Cocteau's *Orphée*), would be encouraging of creativity. Though I would have preferred him to be Maurice.

'Maurice, what does Magda study?' I dared to ask.

'Magda?' he said, with a false air of surprise, as though I had mentioned some stranger, or some public person, about whom he could be supposed to know nothing more than I did. He looked at me as though I had asked a trick question, or at least the wrong sort of question about a woman who was, after all, primarily a woman. I might, his look implied, have been asking him about Grace Kelly or Marilyn Monroe, and expecting some damn-fool answer like 'the art of acting', when everyone knew that these women, famous as they were, had become the sexual trophies of men even more distinguished than they were: a prince, and a playwright. Was it so embarrassing to ask a serious or vocational question about a woman? Was he thinking that I expected him to blurt out that she was studying to become his personal property? His hesitation was only momentary.

'Magda is really a dancer, of course,' he said. 'She ought to get work in one of the London companies, but she doesn't try hard enough. She's very worried about her brother, who she wants to get out of Hungary. She doesn't have any money. She's actually a librarian at the moment.'

Such answers seemed factual enough, if betrayingly like a list, but they didn't answer the question, which had been designed to ask a second, concealed question: 'What is your relationship with her? Do you teach her?' They didn't solve her mystery, either, but no doubt Maurice was deliberately taking me no further than the dons in carpet-slippers were going to get with Shakespeare. I didn't feel that I could ask more. Although it was natural that I might now want to know more about her, it also equally seemed to be a trespass on Maurice's rights over her, whatever these might be, to be asking such questions of him. I would have to ask Mike or Denis or Jim, instead.

13. Paula's Bottom and Margaret's Knees

Paula's world, by contrast, seemed totally closed to me. If she had an entourage of her own I wouldn't have known where to look for it. There were certainly friends who came to the house who were not part of Maurice's world, but I couldn't therefore conclude that they were exclusively a part of hers. They seemed rather to be part of the collective social duty of the family, local spinsters, farming tenants, a retired archaeologist, other fox-hunters. I had the feeling that such people would turn up in any case, whoever lived at Charlwood, and didn't mind who they found there. Many of them were old enough to remember 'the Colonel's days', and a few so old that they probably expected the Colonel (whoever he was) still to be there but were perfectly happy to accept sherry from Paula. Gin was 'the Dudleys'' private drink and reserved for Maurice's friends. The sherry was provided by the Pig, and subject to tedious analysis by him. To see little Miss Adkins, or the Caigers, or Dr West, attempting to engage the Pig in rational and polite conversation was wonderful. Their relief at making sense of his responses was always clouded by the suspicion that they couldn't have quite heard correctly, so that social groups which contained him could always be identified from a distance by the smiling and the nodding and the puzzled frowns.

Paula moved about commandingly on such occasions, with the authority of her attractively dry voice and her ability to act unthinkingly upon her intuition of people's needs. With me it might be propulsion by the elbow and something like: 'You'll want to talk to Freddy Caiger about Adlai Stevenson', to her a perfectly reasonable scenario in view of our supposed characters and the political climate, but one which left us smiling uncertainly at each other and talking about his daughter Pet instead.

'Wild, utterly wild,' he said. 'You'd think she'd been brought up by wolves, wouldn't you, and then given some spit-and-polish in the Trobriand Islands? It's the school, of course. She was perfectly normal when she was ten.'

I soon realised that Pet Caiger's school was the same one that Margaret was earmarked for. Indeed, it was quite apparent that the reason Margaret had badgered her parents to be sent there was that Pet was already there and had brought back the good news. This was the place where a girl's greatest weakness, her parents' knowledge of her history and her true self, counted for nothing. It was a place of infinite opportunity in the experimental discovery of new selves. Better still, it was a place where she might find that her 'true self', that precarious and hard-won identity both nurtured and somehow stifled in the bosom of her family, might after all be an illusion, something that it was quite safe, even exciting, to discard.

Did one ever discard it? I wondered about that. There was something slightly rakish about Fred and Dolly Caiger, as though they had just been rigged out to appear in a play by Noël Coward, that accounted well enough for the character of their daughter. Fred viewed the world with enormous amusement and contempt, justified, I suppose, by the fact that as a stockbroker he dealt at first hand with greed and folly. I think he respected Maurice because he'd never been able to sell him any sort of financial product at all. Dolly seemed to like Maurice for different reasons, disguising it well enough with an immense gruff palliness with Paula.

This business of making do with neighbours is even more irrational than making do with family, I thought. The chance of place, like the chance of blood, makes nonsense of the element of choice in human relationships, which is surely the most civilized way to acquire them. I had not then come across the theory of Goethe, popularised in England by Arthur Clough, which reveals the illusory nature of our idea of personal affinity, dependent as it is, even in the gravest matters of the heart, on what Clough brutally calls 'juxtaposition.' We cannot choose our soul-mates if we have never met them; conversely, we are obliged to accommodate ourselves in all sorts of ways to some, perhaps to most, of those people whom we do in fact meet. In what sense had I truly chosen to adopt Maurice as a mentor? When or how had he chosen Paula as a wife? Were Margaret and Pet appropriate and deserved offspring of their respective parents? Were the parents friends because their children were friends, or vice versa? Pet's brother Ambrose was certainly no one's friend, it seemed. Margaret told me that he had a gun, but I didn't believe her. He was an absence or sour presence on any social occasion involving his family, leaving all the eccentric graces and enthusiasms to his mother and sister. Fred's reserve, and Maurice's waywardness, meant that the two families encountered each other in largely matriarchal circumstances, and Margaret and Pet had inherited the different but equally forceful social mannerisms of their mothers.

It was strange. I could imagine Dolly Caiger holding the advanced educational views that would send her children to a school where classes were voluntary and the sexes mixed on equal terms, and Fred would agree, because getting rid of them, sending them away anywhere, might restore the stereotyped elegance of their earlier married life, and they could then spend infinite hours in the anecdotal limelight of the golf-club bar. I could also see that Maurice might come to think the school a good thing, likely to loosen up the streak of Dudley imperturbability in his daughter's character. But Paula? Wasn't this for her a salvo from the enemy? Hadn't she had Margaret earmarked for Cheltenham Ladies' College?

I would sometimes catch Paula, even in the middle of some mild family altercation, or some buoyant sermon from Maurice, simply staring into space. It was as if she couldn't quite believe in the present and had wandered ahead into the future, to see if it might seem any better. This blankness wasn't, perhaps, all that distant from her usual passivity. Something in the full curve of her lower lip, its accommodating smiling acceptance of things, allowed her to keep displeasure in reserve. But I felt that the displeasure was always, and comfortingly for her, conveniently at hand. It came out in surprisingly sharp things said, without the emotion you would have expected to accompany them, as though a display of emotion would have brought her back, unwillingly, into an open relationship with the world.

'Can I help with anything?' I once asked, when some ferrying of trays of seedlings was coinciding with lunch preparations, and Paula's slightly irritated instructions to Mrs B. were audible across two rooms. I recognised the difficulty of thinking about two things at once.

'Walk with me,' she instructed, like a busy consultant surgeon in an emergency corridor. She gave me a bag of compost that was sitting in the hall. 'Through to the conservatory, if you would.'

Obliging, I said something about my memories of my grandfather's little greenhouse, and that wonderful smell, the thin sharp bloom on the green globes of growing tomatoes which I so loved, and which you never get on greengrocer's tomatoes.

'These are zucchini,' she said. 'Too late for tomatoes.'

I was following her, looking at the liquid strutting of her skirted bottom, and wondering what she would say if I ever had the opportunity to slide my hand down behind the elasticated waist and around the hidden surfaces below.

It was a very wild and outrageous thought, but not one that I was immediately ashamed of. There was a thrill in obliging her terse manner, and I was aware that if she had been nicer to me such lewdness would never have bubbled up into my half-consciousness. I was also reminded that she was in theory (in genealogical theory, that is) 'Lady Paula.' Not that there had ever been any evidence of anyone using such a title. You couldn't with a husband like Maurice. But in my imagination it could easily have complicated my early-Huxley role with a touch of Lawrence.

As for it being 'too late for tomatoes', that was neither here nor there. The abrupt reaction might well have been unconscious hostility. In contrast with Maurice, she seemed impervious to enthusiasms. But oddly enough, it made it seem all the more of a triumph to have evidently pleased her in any way, or to have gained her approval, or even her notice. There were other times when I went out of my way to try to animate that blank businesslike profile with remarks that asked for a kindly response. I never thought to blame it on her toothache.

I didn't know what she thought of my French sessions with Margaret, or if she and Maurice had discussed my giving them beforehand. And as a result of my intimacy with Margaret, I began to feel vaguely guilty in Paula's company, as though she might think I harboured the unconscious ambitions of a suitor, or regularly acquired from her daughter an insight into family secrets. I saw so tremendously much more of Margaret than of Paula that in my mind I was able, as it were, to make a psychological calculation of subtracting Paula's character from Margaret's, to see what was left. To see, in fact, if I was left with a version of Maurice. It doesn't work like that, of course. Human character isn't simply a matter of arithmetic, just as you can't, at the biological level, add the parental faces together to make a third. Or rather, even if the new generation's physiognomies are produced by an amalgam of the old, you can't recapture the constituents by a process of isolation or division. The rich variety, particularly in the distant generations like that of one's own grandparents, is charged with its own inscrutability. There are faces that owe no debts, but are themselves, with fresh force, and fresh individuality.

If Margaret was ever inclined to try her mother's aristocratic ways on me, I could laugh her out of them by exploiting the image she had created for me as a craven hireling. I would call her 'my lady', writhing with camp humiliation like Uriah Heep. This reminded her, I suppose, of the fact that because she actually quite liked me she hadn't the right to talk down to me. There was, I thought, something revealingly ambivalent in the giggling view of me presented to her crony, Pet Caiger, ('Ah, the tutor!') that gave a certain power to my role, not unrelated to my maleness, or at least as much related to maleness as to my temporary impersonation of a teacher.

'Now then,' I would say, in a mock-peremptory manner. 'Strong verbs!'

Equally mock groans.

'I go?'

'Je vais?'

'I shall go?'

'J'irai. I wish you *would*.'

'I would go?'

'You beast! You are a beast, aren't you? You should have gone *ages* ago.'

'I should have gone?'

'Je… J'aurais allé?'

'Bravo!'

'It's the only one I learned. I didn't get on to the others.'

'Never mind.'

'I don't like irregular verbs. Why are they irregular? Like Daddy's tax returns.'

'Are your father's tax returns irregular?'

'I heard him explaining to Mummy that it wasn't a tax fiddle, only an irregularity.'

'Oh, that's all right then.'

'But he still had to sort it out with the Inspector. I thought the Inspector might come to the house to see whether it was a fiddle or not.'

'Not very likely.'

'He might do. Like a detective story. He'd be snooping about on the terrace and then come in through the French windows to tell us who had done it.'

'Who had done what?'

'The tax fiddle. And Daddy would say: "It's not a tax fiddle, it's a—"'

'"—a clarinet"?'

When Margaret laughed, she was inclined to exaggerate the reaction by moving her shoulders up and down ironically. Genuine laughter would give too much away.

'Isn't it what *you* do?'

'What?'

'Fiddle taxes?'

'Good Lord, no. I compute the taxes, I don't fiddle them. I'm the chap prowling on the terrace.'

Since grammar wasn't my strong point (I couldn't explain, for example, these three entirely different roots in the conjugation of the French for 'to go') we usually got on to literature as soon as was decently possible.

After the failure of Maupassant, I perversely tried more poetry. You could take it in much shorter strides, after all, and we had already established that it could mean more or less what you wanted it to mean, or even nothing much at all. And that seemed to be particularly true of French poetry. In teaching it, as I soon discovered, you could offer enormous help with the general or linking bits, and then discuss the really interesting puzzles, which somehow demanded less concentration. Margaret was more interested in catching me out than in solving puzzles, but we had some fun with Rimbaud's 'Voyelles' because it led to some deep discussions about private colour symbolism. My days of the week, for example, included blueish and purplish Tuesdays and Thursdays, a distinctly foxy-brown Friday, a scarlet Saturday and a white Sunday.

'Like Church,' said Margaret. 'That's cheating.'

'I don't see why. Actual churches aren't white, they're grey or brown.'

'I didn't say "churches", did I? I said "Church".'

'Ah,' I said, knowingly, not sure if I was about to offend religious sensibilities. 'You're thinking of purity and innocence.'

'Well, why not?'

'What about blood sacrifice? That would make it red.'

'You can't have a red Sunday *and* a red Saturday.'

'I don't want to. *My* Sunday's white.'

'Yes, but that *means* something. I thought the whole point was that you couldn't explain it.'

Since we had spent almost half an hour trying to explain Rimbaud's coloured vowels, I now had to try to explain what 'explaining' meant, and of course got into a fair tangle. As I also did when trying to compare our own coloured days of the week (her Thursday was orange, for example, and her Friday crimson) and to decide which was better.

'If they're private, then neither can be better than the other,' she insisted.

'Could one set be truer than the other, then?' I asked.

'Of course not,' she said quickly. 'They aren't true at all.'

'Well,' I argued, 'if they aren't at all true, how come we both think that Monday is yellow?'

This was our one point of concurrence, and since we had written our lists on bits of paper, there had been no cheating.

'A coincidence,' said Margaret.

'Or because it *is* yellow.'

'Oh, crumbs,' said Margaret, but whether in despair at me, or at the concept, I wasn't sure.

We tended not to have duplicate texts of anything, unless I had bothered to go to the library. We simply raided Maurice's study. Rimbaud had been the inspiration of the moment, so we were seated side by side on the sofa, looking at it. We decided that his colours made sense because they were categories, and I told her about alpha and omega, but all the time I kept noticing her knees.

I suppose that I didn't see what was in due course to be called a 'mini-skirt' on a grown-up woman until about two years later, when there was a strikingly woolly pink one at a party in New College JCR shepherded about by a friend of mine with the obvious awareness that it was as exotic an animal as an emu. It was a wild harbinger of a commonplace to come. In fact knees were still well-hidden in those days and had an effect that I imagine ankles had on the Victorians.

But if you were a child, then of course you were wearing short skirts in summer, and if you were sitting on a sofa they would naturally ride up and crumple well above the knee. Very much above the knee, in fact. There is something practical about the knee, and because of the kneecap it seems to be a more serious

117

joint than the elbow. It is bulky, flexed, smooth, a little engine of cartilage and bone that divides the useful muscles of the calf with its protective shin from the more leisurely and complex arrangements of the sturdy thigh. Even from behind it looks practical, the little creases at once vulnerable and purposeful. On Margaret's legs, jutting at a casual angle to each other in a beam of evening sun that had slowly encroached upon the room, there was a light savannah of tiny blonde hairs, barely sparser on the knees than below or above them. Next summer she couldn't possibly be found sitting next to me, dressed like that. Perhaps even this summer it wasn't right, and I thought that if Paula should happen to come into the room she would immediately see that it wasn't. But Margaret was unconscious of it, and of everything else, and even let her hand, after she had pointed to some phrase at issue in the anthology I was holding, fall back lightly for a moment on to my own thigh, which somehow seemed a natural and innocent resting-place for it.

It occurred to me that I should try Colette's *Claudine* as a reader. There was something in the character of the heroine that might prove an interesting challenge to Margaret's sense of propriety, a sense of passionate adventure to live up to, perhaps. And I thought that she might like Claudine's relationship with Anaïs, the gawky girl who is always eating pencils and chewed-up blotting paper, and who, as I remembered her, bore some resemblances to Pet Caiger. The novel had been mildly scandalous half a century ago, but would surely not be inappropriate now for Margaret, even though she was markedly younger than Claudine. Did it not have a recklessly lesbian headmistress, I suddenly wondered? Would that be a problem? A friend of mine at school had been found reading Joyce's *Ulysses* and had had it confiscated, an incident that seems astonishing now, but which made one in those days sensitive to the pitfalls of prejudice. When I looked at the Colette, it seemed perhaps too much of a challenge to Margaret's not exactly rudimentary, but certainly short-winded French. Just as Joyce's English was hard enough in its own way to make my friend's eyes glaze over in his triumphant search for the surprising and offensive passages, which he had to admit were few and far between.

Unlike the withdrawn and tractable Anaïs, Pet Caiger was the dominant partner in the relationship. When they were together, it was Margaret who seemed withdrawn, her teasing and sometimes fierce ragging of me forgotten. She seemed in some instinctive way to hand over to Pet, as though Pet had a superior right to interrogate me and mock me. But Pet's mockery seemed to be much more like a challenge of serious intent, designed to force me to acknowledge her as a sexual presence.

You could see the difference in the eyes. Margaret's brought to their interrogation a reflection of the subject of the conversation, a momentary gleam that endorsed a tricky question or underlined a riposte. Pet's eyes searched you out with a generalised penetration that didn't have much to do with anything being said, or not said. Something in them, beyond the twinkle of a joke or the narrowing of a considered answer, maintained that wordless dialogue of the body that is natural to men and women, and beyond their control. It was as though Pet, young as she still was, knew already that she was no longer a child, but could not yet quite believe that she was allowed to be anything else, and looked to me with wordless appeal to tell her who she was. But how could I tell this grubby waif what she was? An embrace would have done it, the prince's kiss ending sixteen years of oblivion to the body and its identity. But she was as far from sixteen as I was, on the further side of that border, and the fairy-tale age with all its legal and social accoutrements lay between us like a theoretical line drawn by field-marshals on a map, creating a dangerous no-man's land between the embattled fronts of opposing armies.

I didn't feel this with Margaret at all, despite the sometimes alarming enticements of her physical presence, largely because she was so unaware. I felt like a sexual spy in her presence, clever enough not to be discovered. With Pet I was recognised, my rank and uniform were proclaimed, the enticing hostilities openly entered into. It made my ridiculous fantasy of goosing Paula seem like pure knockabout.

Was it for this reason, I wondered, that Paula seemed to dislike Pet? She couldn't be openly unwelcoming, of course, but she always put the girl at a frigid distance. It was as though Pet were some sort of inescapable deficiency that accompanied her daughter and best left unacknowledged so as to minimise its effect. Not a person in her own right, but a passing burden of puberty. Not a friend, but a fad. Perhaps even in some irrational way infectious. With Dolly Caiger's anecdotes of difficulties with her daughter, she commiserated rather than praised or reassured. She was glad to recognise that there were problems with Pet. With Margaret, of course, there were no problems. Margaret was a favoured creature designed in her mother's image.

All this, together with the somewhat histrionic attentions of Magda, created a distractingly erotic aura for me, about which I naturally speculated. It entered, with immediate priority, that storehouse of emotions and images which the imagination draws on. I started to write sonnets with fairy-tale settings, in which despotic power, awakened innocence, family concealments and erotic disappointment were all outlined in the distant and decorous charm of fable.

I even wrote one in French to appease my friend Dominique, whom I had been neglecting ('What is the matter with you? dead—mad—or—no hands to write?'). She was polite about its rotten French, and polite, too, about its extemporised quality. It was called 'Liens':

D'un roi vieux et d'une fille de roi ensemble
Je crois les vrais liens d'être l'exil
Loin l'un de l'autre, l'hypocrisie, le bile,
Sang rouge et clair. 'Rire de poupée! Elle semble
Sans respect qui doit cultiver son tremble!'
Evidemment le faux roi sert bien
Ce conte lascif. Leurs lèvres moites, rien
Ne les gene, jamais ils ne se ressemblent.
S'il soit son père les tempêtes peuvent l'aider
Dans les vastes espaces autour de sa tête
Qui tourne en honte ou arrogance. Il sait
Que ce paysage fleuri la rend toute bête.
　　Repentez-vous, mauvais monsieur! Et toi,
　　Termine tes noces qui tuent le pauvre roi!

It was characteristic of most of my poetry at that time to take no trouble to make my meaning clear. This failing is even more apparent in a language not my own. But there is a sense in which for a young writer the language of poetry is a wholly artificial resource in any case. The strange verbal contraptions are themselves like translations of something mysteriously bestowed from elsewhere.

What about this French sonnet? Did I think that Maurice should have lost his temper with Margaret? Did I think that he was sexually jealous of her? Or afraid of her becoming a woman? I'm sure not. I imagine that I simply wanted a suggestive glue for those fragments of pseudo-Rimbaud and pseudo-Yeats that buzzed like irritants in my head. The colourful otherness of fable, and the melodramatic summarising of the sonnet form, pleased me in themselves.

The chaste formality of these poems totally conceals the feelings which contributed to them, I now see, whereas ideas for films that occurred to me at the same time were full of the most explicit and violent symbolism. No doubt this was owing to the quite different models I naturally adopted at the time, for example in poetry, Robert Graves; in film, Luis Buñuel. It was no wonder, then, that I saw a better future for myself in films than in poetry, even though I had as yet to acquire a real 'rhetoric' for film and was not only struggling actually to get the films made but was struggling with my sense of what for me film language really was.

It was at about this time, that's to say towards the end of the summer, that the Pig disappeared. Now there was a subject for a film indeed, if I had had the wit to understand it.

14. Living with the Pig

It seemed for a time an astounding mystery, even if it was, when you thought about it, hardly surprising. Richard Dudley lived already in a world entirely his own, sharing none of it with his family, not even the details of his so-called job with Denzil and Phipps, the genteel Hereford wine merchants. Maurice and Paula didn't even know as it turned out, whether he had to clock in there regularly. After all, it was quite a distance. I got the impression that he was a kind of roving representative, chatting up old biddies throughout the western counties, persuading them to buy his firm's petits châteaux. Could he not now in his suddenly remarked-on absence simply be doing more of that?

Maurice shook his head.

'Unless he has acquired some inamorata who likes him more than his amontillado,' he said. 'Not likely, don't you agree? His things are all here, and his overnight case. That's three nights of wild passion without thinking to let us know or make excuses at Denzil and Phipps. I rang them this morning. They've absolutely no idea where he is.'

The thing was that the Pig did quite often stop over in his travels, when he was making his rounds, as called it, at some distance from home. 'Trying to get the Cornish to drink hock with their pilchards,' he would say. 'Back the day after tomorrow.' But this time he hadn't been seen by anyone since Tuesday and had missed a couple of meetings. Paula blamed the firm.

'They could have told us earlier. They're well aware of his problems. Bill Phipps was probably simply relieved not to have him around for a while and thought he would keep quiet about it. Silly man.'

'It helps being the son of Lord Tewkesbury, I'm afraid,' said Maurice. 'It's a snobbish trade. You have to find ways of persuading otherwise rational people to pay 12/6d a bottle for wine that tastes just the same to them as stuff they can get for 5/- at the grocer's. To that extent, the Pig somehow manages to help them shift their stock.'

It wasn't the only advantage of being the son of Lord Tewkesbury. The local constabulary regularly turned a blind eye to his lapses and escapades, and there was many a time when a grateful case of wine turned up quietly at the police station.

'It's the only rural force in the country which can be relied on to a man to tell you the difference between burgundy and claret,' said Maurice. 'But really, it's no joke. Something's going to happen one of these days. Probably it *has* happened this time.'

Paula became too distraught to show herself, and the whole house had the suspended, self-conscious air of a place where tragedy was brewing. Maurice was upset, too, I could see. He still made jokes, but jokes couldn't restore normality. Mrs B. was openly tearful ('That nice Mr Dudley. Never a hard word for anyone') and it was as though some long-forestalled nemesis had at last caught up with him, something that everyone had feared for him and tried to put out of their mind.

It was only Margaret who seemed oddly anaesthetised. We were still trying *Claudine à l'École*, in my stubborn hope that she could manage some of it, skipping the first few pages about Claudine's love of the countryside and beginning with the departure of the old headmistress, and the smell of the classrooms. I thought that might appeal to her. It was still fairly tough going for her, however, and as usual her attention wandered.

'You must be worried about your uncle,' I said.

She looked at me instead of replying. It was as if she didn't know quite what to say.

123

'I'm sure he's all right,' I said, as convincingly as I could, knowing that she knew they had been searching the river.

'Oh yes,' she said. 'Yes.'

It was strange. It was as though she indeed knew he was all right, but that that wasn't the point. He was all right, but there was still something wrong. I suppose I had an intuition that behind Margaret's apparently unperturbed demeanour was a quite specific anxiety of some kind. I looked at her in deep interrogation.

My feeling that the house was like a stage-set which was prepared for action had come to a sudden alarmed realisation that Margaret knew something about her uncle's disappearance and had been unable to tell her parents. She was still staring at me, in what was now a kind of rictus of terror, as though she were waiting for *me* to make a move, for *me* to tell *her* what I now knew she was going to have to tell me.

'Do something!' she suddenly cried, in a voice that brought shivers down my back. 'Don't tell them! Make it all right!'

I was all at once brought centre-stage in this family drama. I was the recipient of a guilty secret. I was the friendly outsider who could be relied on. I was, perhaps, the inspector we had already discussed who would step through the French windows and explain everything and restore normality.

Even as she told me, bursting into tears, I thought: I'm not up to this, let someone else deal with this. But of course I had to deal with it. 'What is it, Margaret?' I asked.

'He's in the barn! He's in the barn!'

It was obviously for her a great flood of relief to fling herself into my arms, and as I comforted her my anxiety at her critical revelation was strangely confused by the inevitable sensuousness of the embrace. It stirred me to action.

It was soon established that the Pig had been locked in an old barn on Tuesday afternoon, principally by Ambrose Caiger, but with the help of his sister Pet. The barn was part of the Maxwell farm adjoining the Caiger's house but was never used. It was still lockable because its doors had a heavy external wooden bar that could be swung into place. Otherwise it was a remote, neglected repository of outdated and rusting vehicles and implements, windowless, and beyond shouting distance of any public road. Why was he there? Why had he *gone* there (since he could hardly have been taken there, against his will)?

The whole process, that afternoon, of rousing the Caigers, pacifying the hysterics of Margaret, and of Paula, of simply finding the wretched barn, and of getting at all near to it in the car, seemed at once interminable and yet to pass as in a dream.

My principal memory is of the Pig stumbling out into the evening sunlight, blinking and unshaven, into the arms of his sister, who could only say, over and over: 'What have they done to you, what have they done to you.'

One ridiculous detail: before they actually made contact, as Paula began to hasten across the few yards that remained between them, with Maurice looking back at them, his hands still on the opened barn door out of which the Pig had hesitantly come, her brother stood stiffly in front of her, and saluted.

We got him home, but not everything was explained that day by any means. There were abbreviated hints, recriminations and accusations in the car, but the main business was to see that the Pig was all right, and to get him to bed. I made my escape at the same time, feeling in the way.

'Well done, Johnny,' Maurice whispered. 'It doesn't look as though Margaret could ever have got around to telling *us* since she hadn't told us already. What a mess.'

He ran me as far as the bus stop but had to get back to the shambles at home. I didn't blame him, even though I had to wait nearly an hour for my bus.

I ought to be saying that I pieced the story together later, and of course I more or less understood what had happened, but there was an unusual sense of cover-up, I mean unusual in that Maurice had been induced to collude in whatever sanitised version of events had been agreed with the Caigers, and even to me he was less than open. If you make bargains about such a serious issue, you are going to have to close ranks, and the misbehaviour on both sides is going to be played down, or at least equalised. It seemed undeniable that the Pig had discovered Ambrose's secret den, and then had done something so outrageous that Ambrose had felt justified not only in shutting him up there, but in *keeping him there*. He would have to be let out eventually (surely?) but Ambrose could draw on his rich balance of grievance when the account came to be settled. Or maybe he was so angry about it that he simply didn't care. Or had he done it gallantly on behalf of Pet? This was one set of probabilities. Another scenario had the Pig lured openly to the barn by both children, and simultaneously entertained, seduced and tormented for some time. It would account for the apparent watering and feeding of the victim, and for the gradual and inextricable involvement of Margaret, such as it was, something planned that got out of hand. I don't know what the truth was but guessed that the Pig was quite capable of having exposed himself again without it necessarily having meant anything very much, and luckily the Caigers (perhaps prudently in the circumstances) didn't press the matter. Neither side welcomed the drama.

My overriding memory of the affair is that moment of release. The Pig stumbling through the nettles, blinking and unshaven, with loosened tie, then pulling himself together in front of his sister, and saluting her. It was as stiff a salute as in his weak state he could manage, as though he were handing over a regiment.

Was it in some sense an apology? Or was it a self-justification, an involuntary acknowledgement of why he should be in such a mess, a reminder of something? Paula took him wholeheartedly in her arms as I had never seen her embrace Maurice or Margaret. It was a pure Dudley moment, and excluded everything else.

'We never knew what happened to him in the prison camp,' said Maurice, 'but whatever it was, he just couldn't pick up his real life afterwards. His inner life, I mean. But sometimes that absence is too much for him, and it erupts. Do you understand, Johnny? He knows that something is missing, but he has also deliberately forgotten what it was. If he could remember, he might be able to piece it together again. But he can't. He's perfectly harmless. So harmless as to be almost boring. As for Ambrose Caiger, he's a little shit of the first water. Probably thinks of himself now as some sort of hero, locking a grown man up like that, but Richard needn't have stood it for a minute. He only put up with it because he thought he was in the hands of the Japs again.'

When I told my friend Michael about it all, it was his pleasure to dramatise it even further.

'You do realise, don't you,' he said, in his most excited and conspiratorial manner, 'that your madman is really in love with his sister, and she, barely realising it, gives him all the innocent physical release that he needs?'

I laughed.

'Doesn't it make a wonderful story, though?' he went on. 'Your gaunt composer barely understanding what has happened to his marriage, thundering his chromatic octaves in an embroidered dressing-gown, while in a turret on the other side of the castle, fitfully lit by flickering candelabra, brother and sister consummate their lifelong passion in shuddering hugs.'

'You've been reading too much Thomas Mann,' I said.

'If only,' said Michael. 'It's nothing but work, work, work, with Mods looming.'

I visited Michael at Trinity, acquiring some sense of what Oxford might be like when I was eventually to get there. I arrived at dusk on a muggy summer evening (very different from the cold inquisitorial air of my February interview) when the nightly riots had already begun. Beer was poured on me from a little window overhanging the Broad. A man in pyjamas was running along the pavement, bumping into me. He had a pewter beer-mug tied to his pyjama cord. Michael was quite pleased and perhaps even proud that I was shocked by all this.

'These are the people who ran the Corps at school,' he explained. 'These are the people who sneered at us, and were very correct, and wore celluloid collars. Now there's no one for them to impress, so they've reverted to childhood.'

And he added, in an uncharacteristically partisan spirit: 'They're all Balliol men. Just because they were Head of the River last term they've varnished all our lavatory seats. Do be careful.'

I wanted to know what was going on in films.

'Oh, you must ask Rex,' said Michael. 'He reviews them for *Cherwell*. He *is* films here.'

127

Michael had most of his friends round for my benefit. It soon became clear that whatever 'films' may once have been, 'films' had died a death. Rex told me about the grandiose ballet film called *Between Two Worlds* that the Oxford University Film Society had been induced to make, in colour, starring Tutte Lemkow. It was, for OUFS, an overweeningly lavish project, which had finally brought ruin in the shape of bills for optical dissolves and other laboratory effects. The Proctors had put the Society into the equivalent of receivership, and the sleeping Senior Member, who was Lord David Cecil, had even charmingly offered to dip into his own pocket to help out. I was to discover the full horror of the debt two years later, when I became Treasurer and spent most of my energies in paying off the remainder.

No, the general view was that 'films' (except for the latest offering at the Scala, currently *The Rose Tattoo*, which nonetheless must be savagely put in its place) were not on. And it was clear from the general conversation, after my mild tourist's questions were politely fielded, that the only subjects of pressing interest were political.

Oxford had apparently been decisively politicised ever since early May when the philosopher Elizabeth Anscombe had opposed the awarding of an honorary degree to ex-President Harry Truman on the grounds of his criminally unnecessary deployment of atomic weapons at Hiroshima and Nagasaki. There was much amused outrage at the Government's mishandling of every crisis in a year of agonised struggle into the post-imperialist world. There was talk of things I was barely aware of, like the Sèvres Protocol (whereby, when Israel attacked Egypt, Britain and France were able to order *both* sides to withdraw and thereby initiate their own opportunistic ousting of Nasser) and other forms of sinister palliness between the British and French (who had their own share of disasters in Algeria and Indo-China). Michael's friends were scathing about Anthony Eden and Selwyn Lloyd, and full of enthusiasm for the current efforts in Oxford to get penicillin into Hungary (and to get Hungarian students out). When they heard that I was to come up next year, they said:

'You can join the British Universities Volunteer Force, then. It costs £60 to equip a volunteer, exactly the value of your scholarship.'

I was dumbfounded. Was this what Oxford had been like in the 1930s, then, with undergraduates leaving daily for Spain as they now seemed ready to leave for Vienna with £100-worth of penicillin in their pockets? I felt that I was in a time-warp. Or was it simply a long period of the British staring at their own navels coming to an end? I had somehow expected undergraduates to be all disillusioned cynics like Amis-and-Wain, the current comedy duo in the Music Hall of English Letters. Or like Osborne's Jimmy Porter. Or even like post-Kenneth Tynan aesthetes, all wearing velvet cloaks. Michael did sport a green corduroy jacket, which I thought a fair concession to reserve and elegance, appropriate to his character, but the serious students, I soon realised, had been through their National Service and had seen through the national myths that it served to bolster, and one of those myths was Oxford itself.

Over what seemed to be my sixtieth coffee of the day, before I crashed out on Michael's sofa, I raised again my involvement with Maurice, as much to excuse my film mania as anything.

'You don't need to apologise to me,' said Michael. 'Films are your thing, so we'll expect them to be what you do. Don't you find all these politics rather sordid? It's what I always think of as "current events", something you used to get over with at breakfast.'

I wasn't so sure. Weren't Maurice's films self-indulgent? And if they were self-indulgent, what on earth did that make mine?

'I only remember that one of yours with Mr Usborne in it, like the Mad Hatter, and his daughter in a bed in a field, like Alice. I thought it was jolly good.'

Even as he said this, I knew that it was in fact no good at all. But at the same time, my hopes for the new one, the Sidney Peterson-ish one, were still lively. It was just that I couldn't imagine any of his political friends contemplating it with patience. In fact, I would have probably been earmarked with Lord Justice Goddard and Selwyn Lloyd for summary execution. Michael continued to soothe me.

'It sounds as though Maurice Arne is a great find. You must get him to come to Oxford and show his films and talk about them.'

As I went to sleep on this threshold of the new world I was about to enter, I thought that this was very much not the point. Maurice was nothing so trivial as a 'find.' I had no intention of either producing or sharing him. Whenever I was away from Charlwood he seemed vulnerable. My father, I think, considered him something of a musical throwback, and in terms of his background simply a part of Jack's eccentric upper-class world, not to be taken too seriously. Not that my father would have criticized Maurice to my face. Respect for me was one of his many unusual fatherly qualities, and something I didn't always deserve. And Michael's eager Gothic scenario of tempestuous music torn from Maurice's unhappiness within an incestuous ménage, though comic in intention, had a disturbing ring of credibility about it. What does musical feeling in any case derive from?

Had Maurice always been secretly unhappy, to write such tragic music as the Thorold Dickinson film had made famous? What do you take from your life to make the music what it is? What do you go on drawing from it, time after time, like feeding an addiction? I had that melody in my head again and couldn't relate it to the life at all. When you are haunted by a tune it plays itself out in your mind again and again, as though each time there is a new secret to be revealed.

What had Maurice sacrificed to end up living with the Pig, while his wife and daughter careered over Gloucestershire pursuing elusive foxes? And had he become immortal merely because someone like myself couldn't get his music out of my head? It was only by dint of thinking deliberately of other things of no importance whatsoever that I could unhook the music from my brain. But as soon as I had done that and was safely sinking into sleep, the hooting and braying from Balliol started up again.

God, I thought. Was I ever going to survive this tribal culture? It made the crudities and deprivations of the Air Force seem almost civilized.

15. When the Mouse is Away

Summer had been going on forever, it seemed, but gradually I noticed its passing. The girls on the bus no longer had bare upper arms. Orchards were heavy with fruit, the woods with yellowing leaves. I had by now completed much more than half of my service. That moment, when it is daunting to face as much time as you have already put in, knowing how long it has seemed, suddenly became the moment when you have less time to face, and however slight the actual difference, the psychological effect is absolute and inestimable. There was a day when I could say to myself, as I despatched several cooks to BPO 2nd TAF GOCH, that in one year exactly I would be at Oxford, among cavalry twill rather than blue serge, with all this behind me.

In terms of the colour symbolism I had argued with Margaret, I had toiled up the purple and umber crags of my first year and now was descending the emerald upland pastures of my second year into the yellow haze of the valley below. When we are young we endure time, supposing it to contain the promise of future excitements. If life still contains mysteries, we are eager for them to be revealed. If we are to become our true selves, whatever those selves are likely to be, then it is time that we must bring them to birth. But now in age it is the stillness we value, the illusion of time arrested. The moments pass, each holding the promise of being at last entirely the wished-for state of mind, entirely the unanxious stasis of the body, so that there is nothing more to be done than we are doing or have already done. We are incurious about the future. There is nothing about it that doesn't contain somewhere, unnervingly, the seed of that black flower whose inevitable bloom is our death.

The third week of a holiday now seems something much more than the regrettable approach of the end of a special pleasure. It has become a symbol of the accumulated and hastening years of life. At 75, for example, I might be living through the last Saturday of my holiday of life (about 10 am, I reckon, the September sun just reaching the balustrade of the terrace, the sea calm, an enormous butterfly with wings like a pocket-diary lurching momentarily into an orange lily) and I must die biblically when we catch the ferry on Sunday. But look, it is only Tuesday! And don't we now expect to live to beyond the medical average? 80 seems easily achievable, these days. I still feel psychologically much younger than I am, in terms of the real 'holiday', that is—that micro-symbol of the whole. The day itself is a further symbol of such irrevocable passing of time: there is an hour before dinner. The sun has not yet set. Almost anything may still happen!

I wonder if Maurice, coming up to a possible halfway point in his life, still, as it were, at the previous Tuesday, still stumbling from purple crag to emerald upland and back again, had inklings of this feeling? He offered himself to my observation, almost like a timely cautionary example, as the supreme instance of someone who had done much, was still doing it, and planned to do much more. His vocation was clear and settled, and there were no existential limitations upon it. But I didn't know the private man, nor that inner world where desires and fears of an almost palpable kind make the achievements or disappointments of a career irrelevant to happiness.

Among his multitude of activities, he was planning an opera based on *Peer Gynt*. Perhaps, as I now see it, that great sprawling epic of a man's search for his identity and true authenticity was an ideal subject for the Arne œuvre. It would have suited the character of his music perfectly, providing endless opportunity for the modulation of dry humour into more expansive moods of quest, of dance, of dream. And that Nordic frosty quality in much of his music would have been just right for Ibsen. He played me some passages that he had already written ('You'll have to stop thinking about Grieg. Put him right out of your mind') and talked a lot about how a composer should set words so that they can be heard. He said that the poet W. H. Auden, whom he had met on the island of Ischia when visiting the Waltons, told him that only one word in seven of a libretto was ever actually heard and understood by the opera audience.

'Ridiculous, don't you think?' he said. 'It comes of working with Stravinsky, whose English word-hoard isn't too hot after all. It must be dispiriting to send along your sculpted gems of text, "Nature, green unnatural mother..." and so forth, and have them simply steamrollered into the score as though they hadn't been understood by the composer, which they probably hadn't. Now Willie has much the right idea, which is to have as few words as possible. Look how alive the music is when the talking stops, when Troilus and Cressida simply get down to business. Marvellous!'

'Is that why you're so keen on ballet?'

'Of course. It's that business of pruning everything to the essence again. Ballet and opera once belonged to each other, pure dance, pure song, the voice absolutely at its best when it's simply abstracted emotion. Heiala weia, and so forth.'

I knew my *Waste Land*, but I had never heard any of the Rhinemaidens' wordless song vocalised before, and in Maurice's Teutonic falsetto it sounded like a woman getting into a too-hot bath. He obviously admired Wagner like anything.

'It's all in there. Everything. That's why it's such a shame that the poor old boy didn't have the cinema.'

He played me some more of his *Peer Gynt*, the dialogue between Peer and the Button-Moulder.

'Don't say it,' he pleaded, as he shuffled the loose sheets of score on the music stand. 'I know what you're going to say. "He's pinched it from the Master. It's Siegfried and Mime." Well it is, yes, of course it is, but it's my way of suggesting Peer's heroism here. He doesn't consider his life wasted, at all. I've inverted this key phrase here, look, and brought in a modulation of the Solveig motif. He doesn't want to be melted down, and the music tells us why. Do you see the connection between the making of buttons and the forging of the sword?'

I'm afraid I didn't see it at all, but Maurice hadn't needed an answer. His fingers were once more hooked into the keys, hands crossing and plunging in his approximation of the complexities of the score, where the left might have to represent percussion and strings and the right not only the woodwind and occasional brass, but sometimes one of the voices where it overlapped with his own strangulated tenor.

'Ibsen himself lived on Ischia for a time, did you know?' he said. 'I didn't know till Wystan told me. What an extraordinary coincidence, don't you think? I wondered if Wystan would produce a libretto for me, since he seemed to know *Peer Gynt* by heart, but Willie warned me off. 'You'd get too many words,' he said. 'It's not surprising that he has this one-in-seven theory, since he writes seven times as much as is needed in the first place. He helped Willie quite a bit with *Troilus*, though.'

I asked him who had written the libretto. He looked quite sheepish.

'There isn't one yet,' he said. 'I've only written a few set-pieces so far, bits that I know have to be there. It's entirely the wrong way to go about it, I know. Willie suggested Edith Sitwell, but she didn't seem right. The esteemed Dr Dr Sitwell! Well, I mean to say. I've got a real doctorate myself, but I don't use it. "Dr Arne"? That's just asking for it, isn't it? But dear Edith seems to adore her honorary ones. If she gets any more, it'll be ridiculous. No, she's a crony of Willie's, and I thought a touch of the old barge-pole was handy at that point. Paula hated Ischia, too. She thought it was a slum desert. Funny, that. But the sun didn't suit her, of course. Perhaps we should go to Norway, and I could finish the damned thing. I'm going to have to write the libretto myself, aren't I? Much the best thing, really. Wagner had the right idea about that, too.'

These excursions into Ibsen were by way of relaxation from editing his film about Margaret. She and the disgraced Caigers

134

were now away at school, no doubt joining several hundred other near-delinquent offspring of the intelligentsia at the establishment that Maurice had come to call Liberty Hall. I dreaded to think what they were getting up to, and wondered whether Margaret could stand the pace. There was something so safe and solid about her. I imagined her in her muslins and floppy hat on Ischia, kept on a tight rein by Paula, warned away from Auden's flea-ridden cats, not allowed the local wine. But she had been younger then, more obviously a child. Surely Pet would take care of her at Liberty Hall? Or had she felt betrayed in the matter of the Pig? He, too, wasn't to be seen. Maurice and Paula were guarded about this, happy to give the impression that he was 'looking after' Lady Tewkesbury, when it was more obviously his mother who was looking after him. Indeed, I picked up more than one clue which suggested that he was actually in some sort of nursing home.

Paula was often quite short-tempered. She would suddenly appear in a doorway and say: 'Oh, it's you, is it?', in a way which may have been intended to make me feel at home ('You're in this room at the moment rather than in another', or 'I thought it might have been Maurice') but which in my sensitivity to intrusion I easily interpreted as a resentment ('If Maurice isn't with you, why are you here at all?', or simply 'You, yet again?'). But Maurice was happy to leave me in the editing-room while he nipped to the village for tobacco. He smoked St. Bruno, but sometimes the shop had run out. He would return in disgust: 'They only had Digger Shag. Digger Shag! I ask you. How can I smoke something called Digger Shag?'

We did the editing in a little room with an old stone sink that he said was the butler's bottle-washing room. 'We don't have a butler, and we don't wash bottles,' he said, 'but it's ideal for this.' I thought it wonderful to have an editing machine with a viewer, in which you could cut to the very frame desired. I was used to taking a magnifying glass to the strip of film, and simply judging by eye (sixteen separate shots for each silent second of screen time) whereabouts in the confusingly similar succession of images the splice should come. In sound film (twenty-four frames per second) the frames seem more nearly identical, so that the viewer, with handles for forward and reverse winding, is all the more useful. The music had already been recorded, and the score was marked with timed sections of anything between one and perhaps seven or eight bars, with reference to the shots that were to be used in accompaniment. Maurice had a mass of film material and had not always used a clapper board, so that finding the necessary shots as we cut and pegged up the strips of film like washing on a line was quite a rigmarole. Sometimes two strips had to be kept together, marked up with wax crayon for an optical dissolve. The bottle-washing room, with its jungle of dark loops and streamers, seemed like some place of extravagant mourning. When I casually mentioned this to Maurice, he agreed:

'Yes, and here we are like a couple of Fates, snipping away. It's an odd myth, that, isn't it? The spinning of a life, the cutting of a thread. It might occur to any weaving culture, but it's really an analogy with art, that wants a life to *have* a shape, even if it's preordained.'

'But why three Fates?'

'And why female?' said Maurice, in the fake German accent he put on when making one of his frequent psychological remarks. 'Zere you haf a *vairy* interesting question.'

He tried to insinuate that the three female characters who had such power over a man's life represented the women who in fact defined it: the mother, the wife, the daughter. It was only much later that I came across Freud's ideas on this subject, where all possible triads (including Lear's daughters, and the three caskets in *The Merchant of Venice*) are marshalled as evidence for a man's subconscious incestuous choice of his daughter. At least, this is what I took it to mean when I read it, or what I ended up remembering it to mean, probably influenced by thoughts of Maurice and Margaret, and memories of this very conversation. I said that we all had mothers, but we didn't all have daughters. And it wasn't clear what power a daughter had, particularly in ancient cultures.

'Just wait,' he said. 'Remember the hub-caps?'

His motive in making his film about Margaret seemed even more obvious in her absence. It was a claim of power over her, a rite of passage, a sign of release. It was an elaborated version of what the pygmy bushman feared when facing the polished wooden chamber and calibrated tube of a Victorian camera: he had captured her soul. Her escape from childhood was inevitable, but just as she made that final dash for freedom, snip! The film caught her, and preserved her character as his offspring, his possession, for all time. It was like the sash window that comes down and parts Peter Pan from his shadow.

This was clear to me as the film was assembled, since it underlined the theme of possession, both in terms of Margaret's possessions, and of her being in some way 'possessed' by the spirit which haunts them and turns them into symbols of her growing up. Dolls as genitals was indeed the sort of thing intended, and the ticking stasis of pre-pubertal reverie, the sensuous ache of familiar objects, the sense of an inanimate household at play, of a child's dream of adulthood. The music, quite simply for piano alone, was charming but watchful, and a little acid. Its graces contained something baleful, and its gentle tunes were broken and abbreviated. There were conscious allusions to French composers of the turn of the century, allusions to the prettiness and dusty passions of over-furnished drawing rooms. The music had an insistent rhythm, like a slow waltz, evoking nameless yearning and ennui.

It was much more my kind of film than the coy *Symphonie Pastorale*, and I entered on the job of editing it with gusto. Maurice was tolerant and allowed me to make many decisions of montage and timing, but of course, we were not cutting the negative itself. That would only be done when he was satisfied with the edited print, and all decisions could after all be reversed.

'But I might show the rough cut to the grasshoppers to see what they think,' he said.

I had momentary visions of some mystic communion with nature, back to pastoral Thessaly perhaps, with an alfresco projector rivalling the whirring of these critical insects. But Maurice was referring to the Grasshopper Group, a lively London meeting-place of private film-making.

I asked after Margaret, of course.

'When the mouse is away, the cats will play,' said Maurice, musingly. 'Or not much. I think Paula had a vision of a tour of these islands, with guns and golf clubs. There's a hotel in Scotland where you are allowed to take pot shots at small tame birds released now and again into the heather. It works out at about 10/- a bird. But we haven't gone. Really, I seem to be busier than ever.'

I thought it interesting that he should first of all think of saying this. It was obviously what the Margaret situation suggested to him. As though I had said not 'How's Margaret?' but 'How are you without Margaret?'

'Oh, Margaret's having a glorious time at Liberty Hall,' he said, when I persisted. 'There are even horses. In fact, as far as she is concerned, horses are what there principally are. The boys come second. But probably they come a pretty good second.'

I was surprised when he made remarks like these, since being interested in boys wasn't self-evidently a salient part of Margaret's character. It was just the same when he had claimed that she listened to Dean Martin. It was quite possible that she had never heard of Dean Martin, but this was his idea of what his daughter should now be up to. He had captured everything else, so that was it: she could go off now and be like every other girl embarking on her teens. It was purely theoretical now. He would probably expect her to come back from Liberty Hall with Bill Haley 45s, and lipstick. But I really didn't think that was how Margaret was going to turn out. Did he want her to be like that? Did he want rebellion and hub-caps? I saw no sign of it myself. But it seemed to be what he expected.

Sitting with Maurice in the bottle-washing room on successive week-ends, I imbibed a lot of his strange ideas, many of which I suppose have remained part of my own mental furniture, without my quite realising it. Principal among these was his conviction that all life was purely material. I don't mean by this simply that he turned up at church in a different frame of mind from Paula, whose spiritual lineaments such as they were seemed identifiably C of E. In fact, I was well aware that neither of them could be regular churchgoers, since Maurice conducted for my benefit, and sometimes for the benefit of his students, his own cultural services on Sunday mornings at Charlwood, while Paula communed with horses. His conviction was specific. Living creatures, including human beings in all their complex sentience, were obviously made up of nothing else but planetary matter, just as were rocks and trees and streams. Our Wordsworthian feelings for nature were a perfectly credible religion for him, because rationally based on the mysteries of kinship. They constituted an intuition of origins.

The kinship contained precise analogies in some instances. For example, work was the penance of literal rootlessness. When I was slow to see what he was driving at, he would cheerfully make it clear, even while holding up strips of film and peering at them as though their essence were somehow more accessible in stasis.

'It's perfectly simple,' he would say. 'It's so simple that nobody sees it. Unlike trees and plants, animals have no roots. A tree ingests its food in situ, without anxiety. A man, being literally rootless, must labour to produce food. Look at the myths. The Garden of Eden, for instance, with Adam and Eve expelled for disobedience and sentenced to hard labour.'

'God as a sort of magistrate headmaster?'

'If you like. But I'd prefer to think of the old chap as a kind of principle of evolutionary conservatism here.'

'Rather than the principal of an educational establishment?'
Maurice chuckled.

'Certainly *not* the Principal of Liberty Hall!'

'But why do think God is so conservative?'

'Don't you see? God doesn't really *want* to be so repressive. In fact he can't help speculating on the directions his creation might have taken. He's absolutely fascinated by it. Look at the Tree of the Knowledge of Good and Evil. No tree that we know has any such knowledge, does it? Trees have distinctly no choices at all. So?'

He was himself being schoolmasterly again, wanting me to continue his argument.

'So it's not really a tree then?' I ventured.

'Exactly!' pounced Maurice. 'And it gets even better. Not only is the Tree of Knowledge of Good and Evil not really a tree, but Adam isn't really a man, or at least not until he relocates, East of Eden.'

I protested but couldn't help smiling. Maurice pressed on.

'No, the whole point of Paradise is that it is quite a hard place *to get out of*. It's the place where you belong, where you still have roots. The real fall of man is about becoming rootless, isn't it? Then you have to leave?'

'Do you mean that Adam is really a tree?'

'I mean that the Fall is about becoming detached from the planet. And it's about being able to make choices. Freedom to choose. Freedom to be unhappy. And labour as the only means of retaining the contact with the planet that the lost root automatically provided. And are we happy?'

He didn't expect a reply.

'We are full of anxiety and shame, particularly about shitting. Trees don't shit. They take what they need, and that's that. Shit is a great burden, a superfluity. Have you ever seen someone's face when they're shitting? It's agony to get rid of this gratuitous portion of the devoured planet. It needs a rictus of urgent and fastidious shame. But then, when it's over! Ah, that's quite different. The dump has restored us to our origins. It's the contact we have lost.'

There was something wrong with this theory when I first heard it, and I wondered if Maurice was chronically constipated that he gave so much significance to 'the dump.'

'OK,' I said. 'But why aren't we equally ashamed about eating?'

'In some cultures we are,' said Maurice. 'But it is quite different, don't you see? In eating we are actively preparing and re-enacting our lost contact. We dig in the soil. We plant. We reap. That's the primary labour that replaces roots. It's a great joy, then. We are Adam, delving.

'"Delving"?'

'You're not taking this entirely seriously, Johnny. Don't laugh. But you see, that's all perfectly all right, because it is also part of our inheritance to be cynical. We are so tender about our primary satisfactions that we come to be suspicious of them. There's a wonderful remark in Meredith: 'Cynicism—the younger brother of sentiment and inheritor of the family property.'"

'So the family property is Liberty Hall, after all?' I suggested.

Maurice leaned back to roar with laughter, but with an air of wanting to round off the conversation.

'I expect so, I expect so,' he said. 'If that's to be where our choices lead us. But true liberty lies in the stone, which is motionless, or at least motiveless. Freedom to be exactly what it is and nothing else. Growing, and dying: don't you think that all that terrible restlessness must be a grotesque *aberration*?'

At the time I didn't really think so, naturally, but the idea stuck, and I'm not sure now that I see what can be wrong with it. Except that more and more I feel like that older, rather than the younger, brother in Meredith.

16. The Kiss

One day I made the great mistake of telling Magda about the Oxford scheme for funding Hungarian students. She immediately assumed that I would myself leave the country that very week with my pockets stuffed with penicillin. She even wrote out her brother's address on the back of the menu at Prinny's Buttery and tucked the folded card into my pocket. I knew without a moment's hesitation that I wasn't the sort of person to embark on such adventures, even if I were free to do so. I was even for a moment more alarmed at this misuse of the menu, and what the proprietor might say if she noticed, than the prospect of engineering the escape of a political refugee.

'I'm afraid I can't leave the country,' I said, rather lamely. 'I'd be court-martialled.'

'Oh, Johnny!' she said, dramatically lowering her shoulders in despair and looking at me in frustration. 'But who will go, then?'

She made it sound so simple, and so necessary, that it was hard to convince her, not only that, as a conscript, I couldn't possibly go, but also that on the Hungarian side the students were chosen by some committee of the British Council in Vienna and couldn't be whisked out at random in a private cloak-and-dagger process.

There is something about wheedling that is intrinsically counter-productive: the tilt of the head, the mouth that articulates through an irrepressible smile, the insistently intimate tones, these are tell-tale signs of the true motive. Oh, I don't mean that seducing me was her priority. Bringing her brother to England was a serious enough matter, and if his academic credentials were all that she claimed, then it might have been a possibility for him to have been given a Relief Fund Scholarship. I didn't see how I was a credible route to this objective. It was convenient to her programme of humanising me (and eating me up) to make me such a route, in her mind at least. After the crushing of the Hungarian rising no official or civilized arrangements could ever work. It was a free-for-all, with border crossings into Austria to be made dangerously as and when you could (100,000 had achieved it by the end of November). Even if I were free to go, I couldn't imagine what I could actually do. Why didn't he take his chances on his own?

I don't think she had any real idea, either, of what she expected me to do, but she wanted me to play a sort of game of rehearsing the possibilities.

'We will go to the British Council, then, you and I, Johnny,' she said.

I retreated into silence before such impossible plans, and I suppose that my silence unintentionally gave full rein to her fantasies. Maurice told me not to worry.

'She thrives on dreams of every kind, you see,' he explained. 'Like her great career as a dancer. It's her destiny to be hauled out of the corps de ballet and made to dance Giselle overnight, the world suddenly at her feet, and so forth. I think she was mesmerised by that dreadful film *The Red Shoes*. The more unlikely the scenario, the more powerful a hold it has on her. She's happy enough just thinking about it, and she actually makes a perfectly good librarian. I suppose that all librarians, whatever their background, have secret hopes, don't they, with all those dippy novels passing through their hands? Little bureaucrats of the imagination, authorising romance with their purple date stamps. Heathcliff, Rhett Butler, Maxim de Wynter, all of them, on loan for a fortnight. All the masculine attention a nice girl needs, really. Bring him back and exchange him for another. The same thing, but different.'

'I'm sorry about her brother,' I said. 'Will he be shot?'

'From what I've gathered,' said Maurice, confidentially, 'he's the one more likely to be doing the shooting. Don't be fooled. He's much older than she is, and very deeply involved in the black market.'

It reminded me of what Michael had told me about the Hungarian students who were beginning to arrive in Oxford. They couldn't believe that undergraduates expelled by fellow-undergraduates from the University Labour Club for being communists had not been shot instead. 'They're all poets, these Hungarians,' Michael said. 'Life is a tremendously serious business for them. But don't get too excited. They only end up writing long exhortations to Freedom in rather baroque verse, a bit like all those Whig Odes to Liberty in the eighteenth century. It doesn't half make you long for a few more constraints in English society. If I can dare say that sort of thing to a conscript.'

Magda and I did meet in London, but the Hungarian question was avoided because we were all too busy at a Saturday afternoon session of the Grasshopper Group, where Maurice was again showing *Symphonie Pastorale*. At least the topic was mostly avoided, but the good Grasshoppers were collecting, as many people were fashionably collecting, for what had become a 'refugee problem' (£2 for blankets for Hungarians in Austria). When I asked Maurice why he wasn't showing the rough-cut of *Margaret's Dream* as I had thought he was going to, he said, rather unconvincingly I thought, that it wasn't ready. But that's what rough-cuts are, anyway, I thought. There must have been some other reason. Perhaps he was trying to please or distract Magda.

I wouldn't exactly say that she was lionised at the Grasshopper Group, but she was kept in conversation once the film had been shown, since it was (as such groups were) a largely male gathering. The presence of this fey pseudo-star was almost as interesting as the presence of the film-maker—more interesting perhaps, since everyone present seemed to be a film-maker. I began to see that this was how she survived her solitary life. Her small fame gave her self-esteem a boost, and she gained enough courage to play the wan enchantress for a time. But I didn't think her heart was in it. Not really.

Maurice had warned me in advance about the ambitions of some of the more high-profile members like Bob Godfrey and Kevin Brownlow.

'They are commercial rebels working outside the system so that they can retain absolute power,' he explained. 'Bob is making a cartoon film, single-handedly, in the traditional way, *The Siege of Krishna*-something, frame by bloody frame. And Kevin had this brilliant idea of a film that supposes the Germans to have won the War, and Britain now to be a part of the Third Reich. It should have been taken up by a studio, of course, but he'd much rather do it all himself.'

Doing it all himself meant collecting Nazi memorabilia and filming jackbooted rallies in Trafalgar Square at dawn before anyone was awake to object. I didn't know whether this betokened genius or folly. The rushes of *It Happened Here*, grainy, naturalistic, full of sharp-angled details, and apparently 100% authentic, suggested the former. But it was easy to see that the young Brownlow would be superannuated by the time the film could be finished. The bits of Godfrey's cartoon that could be screened were tremendously inventive, much better than any other British animator that I could think of.

On that particular afternoon there was the inevitable Group business, speeches, tributes, the showing of rushes. But then came the films. Brakhage again, full of manic aimless activity; Norman McLaren's pixilated *Neighbours* (the Canadian McLaren was the esteemed theoretical Patron of the Grasshopper Group); Maurice's film; some Frank Stauffacher; and Willard Maas's *The Geography of the Body* and *The Mechanics of Love*. Although the latter showed a full-frontal female nude (hardly to be seen on the screen at that time) and was ostensibly a series of visual metaphors for sexual intercourse, it was one of the most unerotic films I have ever seen. Better was the verse commentary by George Barker to the first Maas film, a kind of microscopic nude travelogue, which was of a different imaginative order to the scissors, locomotives and breaking waves of the second film.

'Is that what you call rhetoric, Johnny?' asked Maurice, perhaps with a memory of the train going into the tunnel in my example from Hitchcock.

'If it is, it's the rhetorical equivalent of a sermon,' I replied. 'I preferred the one with the Barker poem.'

'A bit like Whitman, don't you think? But without the expansiveness?'

'Quite so,' I said, and Maurice roared with laughter at my imitation of him. He took my arm, and lowered his voice.

'What do you think the Grasshoppers make of Brakhage, eh? This one seemed to be about the sex war, what you could see of it. Can he never focus his camera? Do you think this enlightened audience liked it any more than the good burghers of Cheltenham did? Or do they just pretend to?'

'I don't know,' I said. 'You know them better than I do. Wouldn't some of them be happier at Pinewood? And what about you? Do you like it, or do you just pretend to?'

'It's very *simpatico*, naturally,' he said. 'And you can't ignore what the Americans are doing, can you? It was the French before the war, and now it's the Americans. But when you think of what the British might be doing...'

'I didn't know you were so patriotic.'

'No, but really. We're very good at doing documentaries, but everything else is at the level of *Punch*. Massingham going to the dentist and so forth.'

'Comic realism, you mean. Ealing comedies, *Lucky Jim*?'

Maurice's eyes gleamed beneath their Demon King eyebrows with a sort of jolly hatred, and he wiggled his elbows in his characteristic manner.

'That sort of thing. So dingy, really. And so facetious, don't you think? *Three Men in a Boat*. I'd much rather have the Marx Brothers.

I said that I would, too, but at the same time I knew that I really liked both.

After tea with the Grasshoppers I was expecting to continue my 48 at home in Blackheath and was preparing to head off for the Bakerloo Line to the Elephant. I was under the impression that Maurice would be returning to Gloucestershire. Why was I under that impression, I wondered? I had forgotten.

When I asked him, he said:

146

'No point. Paula will be sleeping it off after the extraction of her wisdom teeth. I'll catch the late train and cheer her up in the morning.'

And he thereupon made a great thing of taking Magda and me off to see a young Australian composer he knew, who might come out to dinner with us. He made me feel I had to come as well. Since I had left my arrangements pretty vague with my mother (surely to her great irritation) I was perfectly glad to stay on, but at the same time I felt a lurch of guilt. I had suddenly remembered a crucial conversation that morning.

When I'd arrived at Charlwood, Maurice wasn't yet back from the college, and Paula was about to set out somewhere herself.

'God knows where he is,' she said, pulling on her gloves. 'Will you tell him to pick me up from the dentist? The surgery just rang to remind me that I won't be able to drive after the extraction.'

'Goodness,' I said, wondering if she knew that we were shortly going to London. 'That sounds a bit grim.'

Paula laughed bitterly.

'Not as grim as having them in my mouth. Tell him I'm leaving my car at the Whites, and Elizabeth is going to drive me into Hereford after lunch.'

These were hardly very complicated arrangements, but they must have essentially passed over my head. All that was really in my mind was that there was surely hardly time to fit everything in. In fact, there certainly wasn't. Maurice must have forgotten. And I myself forgot to say any of this to him.

Perhaps if I had conveyed Paula's message, he would have called off the London trip altogether in order to be with her and look after her.

And that might have been somehow absolutely crucial to their relationship just then.

Or it might not.

There are these little moments, sometimes barely noticeable, or arriving quite without warning, when what we choose to do matters enormously. And the choice, if indeed it is presented as a choice, usually seems quite immaterial at the time. Had I feared that the promising jaunt to the Grasshoppers might be called off if I reminded Maurice of his husbandly duty? Or if it wasn't simply that I wanted Maurice all to myself as usual, did I think that I was assisting him in an escape from Charlwood, providing cover perhaps for a day (and as it turned out, possibly a night) with his protégée? Hardly, since I must at that stage have suspected that Maurice was somehow trying to transfer Magda's attentions to me.

But to a nineteen-year-old the significant life model is rather one of escape from attachments, and it suited my notion of Maurice to equate Paula and Charlwood with a sort of duty and routine that might be crippling to the creative spirit. All the exciting side of his personality, his clowning, his weird films, his clothes, his jokes, seemed to spring from a neglect of duty, and for the sake of art I instinctively knew that all of it must be encouraged. Behind my frigidly polite conversations with Paula was a puzzled fear of her as a strong woman who could reduce Maurice's precious world to the status of ridiculous play if she wanted to. She possessed, in a household version of the Cold War, a terrifying armoury of common-sense and scorn which she might never actually dare to use, but which defined the domestic status quo and was carefully stock-piled by her to protect what she knew was otherwise a crippling cultural impotence. And Margaret was entirely in her sphere of influence, an unrebellious class possession, principal satellite of the Philistine Bloc. But this couldn't last for ever. The once unconsciously happy Puggins must make her own choice of life, and become the real Margaret, like a Slav nation in revolt.

I don't think that there was anything remarkably wicked about our evening in London, although it blurs in my mind with later evenings in Soho in the company of my Oxford friends, when enough would be drunk to make memory uncertain, and the experience itself ripe for suppression. Do I now remember strange stories about some of the people we met, and have I unconsciously given myself a role in them that I didn't play at the time? I have always found it easier to stand on the sidelines and observe, than to take action when action offers itself to be taken. It's even easier to stand on the sidelines and notice almost nothing at all, or at any rate to miss the crucial pass, or the actual whereabouts of the ball.

All that I've remembered of Maurice seems to have fallen into the pattern of a story of a sort, but my fund of memories contains much that contradicts the sense that I have tried to make of them, and they are not always precise, or easily located in time or place.

When, for example, was I very drunk in a lavatory, staying locked in there rather too long? Was it Maurice or someone else who climbed round to a window to see if I was all right?

And when was it that I saw that kiss? It is one of my sharpest images of Maurice, and yet it seems to have no place in what I have written about him, probably because the girl was nobody in particular and therefore not a part of what you might call the story. It could have been on that occasion in London, or it could have been anywhere, perhaps even among airmen and airwomen, since Maurice did come at my invitation to Innsworth, out of friendly curiosity. It may have been at a party after the Christmas pantomime that had been organised and directed by an agreeable but vague WRAF officer who was always accompanied by a spaniel with paralysed back legs and a little cart for its bottom. She had heard of Maurice Arne and wanted to meet him. There was something of a party after the party, and I had seen a civilian girl wandering about, attached to no one, looking as though she might have come in off the street. She approached Maurice as he was turning and crossing the room and lifted her lips to his mouth as naturally as she might take a crisp from a passing bowl.

The insolence of natural appetite, carelessly displayed in public, was not more shocking than this apparently arbitrary choice of object and its merely momentary attraction. To be kissed, or to wish to kiss, is a significant private negotiation with one's own body as well as with another's. Observing a kiss removes all sense of that deliberation and yielding, and all that one is left with is the absurdity of the physical contact itself and the inexplicable choice. There is a deep discomfiture in such voyeurism.

As the girl's mouth left Maurice's, his rather large bevelled lower lip was pulled down briefly by the contact, as it might be by cigarette paper, slightly damp and to be peeled from the skin. I thought his mouth then, and in particular his wide upper lip, to be gross in its presumptuous acceptance of such a free contact. It was operating in a quite different mode from its purveying of obiter dicta, or from its smiling, or from its pursed reception of a gin. It looked to possess an arrogant assumption that such attentions from another mouth were, though unlooked-for, part of its due reward for existing at all. It need not stoop with any real interest of its own, but it need not reveal indifference, either. In its recognition of the situation it was merely being practical, and perhaps a little smug. It was demonstrating an absolutely unconscious greed. I have seen people eat sherbet lemons or skewered prawns just like that.

And anyway, I didn't want to see other people, particularly not Maurice, kissing. The objection isn't prudery, but jealousy: if there's any kissing to be done, it shouldn't be done by others, but by oneself. In the case of Maurice this was compounded by what was, I suppose, a kind of condescension in my view of his marriage or of his music. If he was a naturally free spirit, trapped by convention, then he was allowed the inspirational outlet of romantic attachment, and I had become familiar enough with Magda's powdery charms to see their likely relationship in this sort of light, and as being somehow beneficial to her, as well ('She actually makes a perfectly good librarian'). When Magda was fumbling in her bag, or giving little cries of self-deprecation, I could see no threat in her. She needed some inspiration of her own, after all.

But the kiss with the anonymous girl was another thing entirely, and it opened a world of purely sexual opportunism that in my eyes reduced and distracted Maurice from his higher purposes. Perhaps he was like this all the time. Perhaps he was even a predator, and I hadn't twigged. Or maybe he was just putting into operation his own Master Proverb of the Cautious Man. If so, hadn't he realised that every man in the room was doing so, and the girl simply wandering about in a drunken haze and blithely taking advantage of it?

17. The Clock starts Ticking

Winter didn't suit Charlwood. There was an inconsiderate wind that got into everything. There was no more lazing, no more Dagwood sandwiches or afternoons on the river. Margaret came back from Liberty Hall with an air of secretiveness and a notable disinclination to continue her innocent flirting with me. She and Pet took to wearing black lipstick and disappearing conspiratorially, as though they had somehow found nightclubs in the back streets of Gloucester. Maurice was certainly wrong about Margaret being more interested in the school's horses than in the boys. Probably the school didn't even have any horses. Her pony Danger was much neglected, and there were naturally no more French lessons.

Paula was now without her brother and without the equestrian companionship of Margaret. She seemed distant with Maurice, and positively hostile to me. I had tried to get her to come to the pantomime with Maurice, as I thought it might amuse her to see me as a can-can dancer, and perhaps because some sort of pacification and self-abasement on my part was due. But she wasn't interested. (It was also, I vowed, the positively last time that I was going to be induced to wear drag).

I don't think she was interested in me at all. Perhaps I was only the latest and most irritating of Maurice's acolytes. Perhaps she saw right through me as a cover for his adventures with Magda. I tried to make sense of my relationship with her in the light of something that Hugh Arne said to me when I saw him at the Wigmore Hall at the première of the Arne viola sonata.

He was heated, erect, rigid with the exertions of the occasion, nodding at friends who came to congratulate him, but apparently elsewhere in spirit. It was all the more alarming, therefore, when he took me aside to make sure that he wasn't overheard and said, in an unerringly amiable tone of voice:

'I see that you're still hovering. Well, that's really not a good idea. I suggest that you leave them alone.'

I was deeply embarrassed at this and was aware of flushing. I had enjoyed the performance, was thrilled to have been invited, and had said so, and had been expecting some musical confidence, even some acknowledgement that we had once happily played together. And here was this icy rebuke.

Had I heard it quite correctly? What had I done to deserve the accusation of 'hovering'? Who had complained about me?

The milling well-wishers would probably have prevented much of a conversation if I had been able to think of anything to say. To make it worse he gave me a frigid and dismissive smile, quite the most schoolmasterly gesture that I had seen from this very schoolmasterish man, and turned away to greet Maurice, who had been to fetch (how typical of him) a clutch of spilling wine glasses, held in an ingenious way against his chest with curled knuckles and guiding crooked thumbs.

I suppose that at the time I partly suppressed this gratuitous advice (and its implications) in natural self-protection. But even now I don't know quite what he was implying. That he knew their marriage was going through a bad patch? Obvious to me, in hindsight. That I was a temptation to Paula? Ha ha. That I represented the more frivolous of Maurice's occupations and was preventing him from writing music? Surely not.

I didn't understand it, this protection of brothers. Paula embracing the ruined Pig. Hugh being moved to speak cruelly to me in clipped tones, despite an innate shyness that he must have known I shared. It was an alarmingly instinctive loyalty. There was no one like that to be loyal to *me*. Even Magda's single-minded plans to evacuate her brother, putting all her other desires on hold, seemed in its hopeless intensity to possess a nobility that I could barely comprehend. Other loyalties weren't loyalties at all, merely habits or appetites.

1957 dawned with an eloquent communication from Dominique. She knew it was my birthday.

'Premier jour de l'Année 1957
Commencée à 12h sous un bouquet de gin, avec un baiser
      pour tous les fantômes absents
Avec un baiser pour les espoirs
      pour les désespoirs
Avec un baiser pour cette année qui vient
Premier jour de l'année avec une pensée pour un certain
      Niccolo Machiavelli faux ou vrai homme aux
      circonvolutions cerebrals immenses et cruelles
Bonne Année mon cher John
J'ai lu l'histoire of the Lionfaced Man
S'il vous plait
      Laissez votre cerveau tranquille et écrivez avec le cœur—
Vous cherchez beaucoup trop la perfection Monsieur Paul
      Valéry-Lautréamont.'

And more in the same vein. Another rebuke! Although this essentially friendly greeting was a timely and admonitory one, I don't suppose that I took it much to heart at the time. Why had she coincidentally appropriated Maurice's favourite drink in order to risk telling me a truth about my artistic self? Too much frantic brain-work, she was saying, too much surrealism, too much calculation, and not enough heart. But all these things were French, after all! God, was it I who was Macchiavelli, or was she perhaps suffering from another Lycée set-text? Could she be right? She hadn't understood my French sonnet, but why should she, when I barely understood it myself? Maybe she thought it was about her. And she clearly hadn't understood my story *The Journal of the Lion-Faced Man*. This was about a hideously deformed circus

153

performer emigrating on a liner to find the perfectly normal life. The period was Edwardian, and the lion-faced man's sensibility, elaborately exposed in his journal, was a combination of Henry James and Kafka. He is befriended by a busybody called Drummer, who persuades him that he will be more readily accepted by the other passengers if he comes out of retirement and 'performs' at the ship's ceremony of Crossing the Line. The result is disastrous in every way.

The longing for the perfectly ordinary unselfconscious life, the righteous claim made by a reserved personality upon the experience which his deep timidity and scepticism tells him is not after all his to claim, seemed to me (I suppose as much from my current reading as from my own experience) to be a supreme subject for fiction. How can you deserve to be happy, to be commonplace, to accept unthinkingly the opportunities that your immediate desires inevitably put in your way? The lion-faced man is easily persuaded that there is no future for him as an Australian sheep-farmer largely because he is an offspring of Gregor Samsa and Lambert Strether, though he doesn't know it.

It makes me wonder how a delightful monster like Maurice figured in this scenario. Was he someone who had it both ways, had already, as it were, made his move as a sheep-farmer but retained his difference, his mystery, his critical alienation from real life? If so, he was in a supremely powerful position, and for his brother Hugh to perceive me as a sort of Drummer, seducing him from his family or from his art (and it could hardly be both!) was a calumny.

But I was still young and was used to being put down.

After that, and after the fall of Eden, I felt that I was on the downward slope to demobilisation and Oxford, a slope in Rimbaudian terms that was purplish-brown and flecked with greenish sunlight, a year of turmoil resolving itself into something a little more stable. I didn't want to be a nuisance (who had told Hugh that I was a nuisance?). I didn't want to have Magda foisted on me. What would I do? Take her on my arm to Blackheath, and see her sitting on the sofa in her knicker-coloured dress with its funny little ribbons on the side talking intensely to my father and mother about auditioning for John Cranko? I wasn't ready to cope with such a relationship, if one was indeed on the cards. I'd much rather have made Margaret's Three Stooges film, and the odious Ambrose could have been the third Stooge for all I cared, since Annie seemed to be out of favour. Ambrose hadn't returned from his own, more conventional school, but was off skiing somewhere, practising his broken voice. Pet and Margaret had their own fish to fry, and Margaret never produced her promised script.

Maurice himself seemed to be busier elsewhere. No more work on *Margaret's Dream*. So I held off a bit, and waited to be particularly asked. And wasn't, very much.

For a time, I used to wonder if they were happier now, without the Pig, and more or less without Margaret. Had those bits of the past and the future been a distraction from the marriage, or an essential part of it? I wondered, too, in an extraordinarily selfish way, I suppose, if Maurice was happy without me? He had that knack of making you feel important at the point of contact when he lit up with genuine interest. It was impossible to believe that he could simply switch that interest off.

Or was it, after all, I who had switched off, afraid of Hugh or of something that I hadn't myself observed in Maurice represented by Hugh? Afraid of Magda? The more I stayed away the less I felt welcome, and something of this estrangement was my own doing, I soon felt.

Michael said I was well out of it, and that the insatiable Paula, frustrated of her incestuous infatuation, would have inevitably turned to me. Jack, rather irritatingly, bothered to let me know that they had all found me 'charming.' *All* of them? Did that include the Pig? And what about that tense, 'had'? It sounded as though the clock had started ticking in the forest at last, and that perhaps some gracious piece of dutiful hospitality was finally over. It was an unwelcome wind of reality. I didn't want to have been charming. And I certainly didn't want it at all to be over.

Encountering Mrs Rivers at the King's Lynn Festival and discovering her to be Margaret, was, therefore, in its sheer unexpectedness, entirely dumbfounding. It had such a remarkable air of design, that had I been a religious person I might have suspected that I was now completing the final part of some long pre-arranged test of character. It seemed as if clues as to its original nature (erotic opportunities put in my way, artistic choices to be made, even political challenges of a kind, all at a moment of crucial immaturity) were now put into perspective, first by my casual rediscovery of Maurice's concerto and then by the emergence of his daughter into my oblivious and busy life. Each in themselves quite unlikely, but together, wholly distracting. I didn't want to be distracted. I don't think I wanted to know what the test might have been.

My present life, I was convinced, now contained nothing at all of that Arne world of half a century ago. Its familiar lineaments marked me as a cautiously developed survivor of my own personality, as is the case with all of us, I'm sure. But though I am still a writer, I hadn't become a film-maker. Surrealism had been a passing phase. And in my very modest rage for life I now had reason to believe that I was among the happiest husbands, fathers and grandfathers that there could be.

There was a part of me that just wanted to drive straight home after King's Lynn, as I always did on such occasions, simply to re-establish as quickly as possible the private self that had had for a time to be put on hold. And of course I was pretty tired, too. But curiosity got the better of me, and in the end I couldn't resist making the detour into Runcton St. Peter to search out 'Mrs Rivers', wondering what this unconvincingly aged and accoutred simulacrum of the twelve year-old girl that I once knew could possibly have to tell me after all this time.

18. Mrs Rivers

'When they got divorced,' Margaret said, filling up my glass with more of the soapy Chardonnay that I had been nervously gulping, 'I naturally saw much more of Mummy than I did of him, didn't I, Charlie?'

Mr Rivers was an entirely subdued, but self-possessed and smiling man with a brushed-up moustache and a paisley cravat. He raised his own glass in cheerful acknowledgement of the question but said nothing.

'Charlie's not really interested,' she went on. 'The first time he met Daddy, he thought he was a Beatnik. The oldest Beatnik there ever was, didn't you, Charlie? You said that.'

It wasn't an accusation. She seemed quite pleased that he had said it. Charlie Rivers beamed and hummed slightly in agreement.

'That was the fatal influence of Mapleleaf, you see,' Margaret continued. 'Everyone thinks of it as terribly folksy, all Shaker hymns and apple-pie, but it was a den of iniquity, really. You know the sort of thing, I'm sure. Orgies in the log cabins. Hashish fudge. Daddy was such a charismatic teacher, and the students were all over him, but they never let him perform his own music. Not really. He would say: "Why on earth did they ask me, then?" and there wasn't any answer to that. No one ever said. The big thing he was working on would have been perfect. It was based on

Francis Parkman, you know, *The Oregon Trail?* An American subject? But they never performed it!'

'Too long,' said Charlie Rivers, breaking his silence for a moment.

'It was enormously long,' said Margaret. 'He broke all his own rules and included everything. But that was the point. He wanted everybody to have a part. It was written for Mapleleaf as it was then. Anyone who could make a sound, any sound at all. If the janitor had a ukulele, you know? No auditions. Massed choir, the whole campus. It was a principle with him, and why not? I would have thought they would have jumped at it.'

'Money,' said Charlie, eloquently.

'Well, there was never enough money,' said Margaret. 'Do you know what his salary was? When he went out there it was only six thousand dollars. It was ridiculous. You were supposed to grovel, just because they'd once had Copland, and Copland didn't stay long, you can be sure of that. I never liked America. But look, you can do a lot without money. It only needed the will to do it. He didn't have any allies. He needed allies. Didn't he ask you to go out there? I thought he tried to get you a visiting Fellowship?'

This thought was a fantasy of hers. Or was it? Perhaps it had been a fantasy of Maurice's. If I'd been asked to go, I would have remembered. Wouldn't I? But vaguely at the back of my mind was a lurch of potential guilt. Had I been asked, made a cowardly refusal and then forgotten all about it? Had I even kept vaguely in touch for so long, and then forgotten about that?

'After Uncle Richard killed himself, my mother really went to pieces until she was saved by Stephen Stanger. She had a happy life with Stephen, I would say. Daddy hated him, of course, though he cultivated a great air of pretending otherwise. He was rather good at that. I suppose I disliked Stephen, too. All water under the bridge now. Stephen died of cancer in 1997, Mummy the following year. I couldn't get Daddy to come to her funeral. I did try, but he was already quite disorientated. Perhaps you couldn't blame him. The betrayers and the betrayed are never quite confident of identifying each other, are they? He was the one who was alone.'

On and on she went, returning to the defence of the parent she clearly felt she had in fact most neglected. She was remembering my Charlwood days, I'm sure, and trying as best she could to bring me up to date with the Maurice that I remembered. It was soon apparent, however, that it was her own life that was uppermost in her mind. It had proceeded in a course that I could easily have predicted: minor troubles with the remarried Paula, troubles with her grandmother and money, some foreign travel, life in London as a posh PA, marriage to Charlie Rivers, a financial advisor who had now taken early retirement and seemed to play a lot of bridge and golf. The house was obviously the best house in Runcton St. Peter and had had a lot of money spent on it, but the life going on inside it was of the most mundane imaginable. Craft-shop lithographs and framed photographs. What could I ask her? Did she have horses? Did she still ride? Could she speak French? The little girl I had known was a million miles away. And yet the poise and insistence and directness did remind me a bit of the young Margaret.

But of course, what I really needed to ask her was the crucial question about Maurice, the one that I had not wished to know the answer to when I had looked him up in the old Grove. I knew that I had been superstitious about it. Quite a silly thing, really. If I didn't find out that he was dead, then perhaps he wasn't yet dead. But what would that mean? I knew almost nothing about his later life. There were thirty years or more after the Mapleleaf period to account for, with some crusty semi-superannuated position at the Royal Academy of Music, I gathered. Thirty more years of not getting his stuff performed, perhaps. Thirty more years during which the students became less interested in him. Years during which whatever fame he once had would fall away like leaves from a winter tree, never featuring in the Proms, leaving his passing more or less unremarked. Margaret talked and talked but told me nothing that seemed to enlighten me. If I didn't ask the direct question soon, it would be too late, and the ensuing awkwardness would be even harder to handle than all the meaningless information on offer.

'And Maurice himself,' I said tortuously. 'Did he, is he…'

'He's still miraculously in the land of the living, if that's what you mean,' said Margaret, with a touch of irritation. ''97 in November, can you believe it. Do you want to see him?'

I was quite alarmed at this. She said it in such a sudden and casual way, that I half expected her to open a cupboard door and reveal him hanging there in a state of readiness for display to casual visitors, like the stuffed Jeremy Bentham. I felt a sudden surge of emotion, a combination of bewilderment, old affection and pure fear.

'You can see him,' she said. 'But he's not well. In a way, that's the reason I turned up at King's Lynn. I was sort of putting two and two together. Dotting i's and crossing t's if you like. Charlie said I shouldn't.'

Charlie looked down at his glass.

'But all his friends are dead, you know. No one goes to see him. There really isn't anyone. But there is you.'

'I'd love to see him,' I said, not knowing whether I meant it. I think that I had truly presumed that he was dead.

'It's near Norwich,' she said. 'Not far, really. We can go in the morning.'

However far Norwich was (not exactly near), the proposed event suddenly took on the urgency of fact, beyond demur. My mind raced.

'You can stay the night, of course,' said Margaret. 'There's some cold supper. I've laid a place for you.'

It was one of those hijackings that soon become impossible to argue with. Margaret had become a manager. She managed Charlie, and it seemed that she continued to manage Maurice. Now she was managing me. I could ring Prue and tell her that I'd be home tomorrow. I already had overnight things for King's Lynn. Visiting Maurice was a last chance, Margaret intimated, somehow important for him. Despite my initial objections, I had no ultimate defence to any of this. It was settled.

Supper was a further account of the unexceptional life of Margaret and Charlie, and of their children, now pretty well scattered over Europe, working for UNESCO or making neutrinos perform in underground laboratories, and themselves having given birth to one or two quite unimaginable offspring.

I had to give an account of myself, too, of course. Margaret's directness and assertiveness seemed to me to be performing beyond the requirements of the occasion, as though this were a formal dinner party long prepared for. All the time I was trying to relate her to the girl I had known those many years before. She had been thoroughly independent then, challenging to her father, not particularly cooperative with me in my strange schoolmasterly role (why should she have been?) and replete with mysteries in the privacy of her own life. This belated appropriation of me had come from absolutely nowhere. I tried to ask her why she had sought me out and didn't get any sort of answer. I think she had seen something I had published, and it had engaged some gear in her mind. She even attributed the move in some way to Charlie.

I telephoned home and explained the unlikely situation as best I could and became resigned to another day away. My fatigue kicked in thoroughly and locked itself into my right temple. Large glasses of Australian merlot didn't help. Charlie had imperturbably moved on to whisky. I was glad to be able to plead my exhaustion convincingly and soon enough retire.

19. A Little Sympathy

I had used the bathroom, and was still nosing about my guest room, in the way that we do, picking up clues about the lives and tastes of our hosts when there was a tap at the door. It was Margaret in a quilted dressing-gown, holding a sheaf of papers.

'Can I come in?' she whispered.

I could hardly say no.

She closed the door behind her in a slightly ominous indication that what she was going to say wasn't for the ears of Charlie. Perhaps he was still at the whisky. Or even asleep. I was aware that I had been followed upstairs by both of them after a short interval.

'When I saw that book of yours,' she said, 'something about finding a journal in an old piece of furniture, wasn't it, I got the idea of looking for some things I remembered I had somewhere in the attic. We had a great clean-up after Charlwood.'

She had already explained the curiously archaic entailment of Charlwood, whereby on the expiry of Paula's lifetime interest it passed either to her son, or to the male heirs of a younger sister I knew nothing about. When I commiserated, Margaret had been dismissive, as if the house were a trivial element in the general complexity of inherited wealth and property. No doubt the intention in any case had been to protect it from falling into the hands of the likes of Stephen Stanger, even if much else had done so. I wasn't greatly interested in the tortuous machinations of money managers. Money always has ways of protecting itself, and the fact that Charlie was in that business himself was typical of the fact. Margaret had certainly not fallen on hard times.

'It's not easy finding somewhere to store the past, is it?' I said, thinking of all my father's papers, which I still had in filing cabinets in my study.

'Daddy wanted his archive to go to the Academy and to the British Film Institute, so we arranged all that while he could still think about it. Just in time, really.'

She was standing a little close to me, I thought. I had the opportunity to observe that discreet texturing of the skin of cheek and neck in a healthy woman of nearly seventy that it would be cruel to call wrinkles. Her hair was expensively layered into an effect that could be called neither blonde nor grey. The eyes were bright, the teeth well kept.

'Anyhow,' she went on, 'I found this.'

She gave me the sheets of paper, held together by a rusting paperclip. They were sheets of typing paper of an old-fashioned kind (foolscap quarto, as I knew from my printing days, put out of business when A4 was introduced) covered with uneven childish writing in pencil. There was a heavily underlined heading: 'The Three Stooges at the Dentist.'

'So you actually wrote it!' I said. 'I've never seen this.'

'You disappeared,' she said. 'I came back for the holidays and you'd gone. Daddy said you'd had to go on a fire-fighting course before you left the Air Force.'

'But that was much later,' I said. I had a sudden memory of something I had quite forgotten: trying to control the powerful jet of water that surges out of a one and three-eighth nozzle on the end of a rearing fire-hose gripped tremblingly under your arm.

'Later than what?' said Margaret.

For the moment I was confused. More than one overlapping telescoping of time was too much for me. But it must have been Margaret who was confused, skipping at least one period of holidays when we might have made the film. Her having after all

163

bothered to write some sort of script was more than touching. It seemed to change her entire attitude to me as I had then supposed it to be. She had once imagined us still doing things together.

'It's funny how we all remember different things,' I said, by way of a general excuse.

'Do you remember staying with us when you were taken ill?'

'No, I do not,' I said.

'Daddy knew your commanding officer and rang him up. You weren't all that ill, but Daddy made a great thing of needing to look after you. I think he rather liked interfering with military procedures. Perhaps you'd simply had too much to drink. I expect he certainly had.'

'Sorry, I don't remember that at all.'

I didn't remember it. Or I was determined not to remember it. Wouldn't I have remembered it just as much as a fire-hose?

'Oh, Johnny,' she said, in rebuke. Her use of this name was making me feel much younger than she was herself, and it embarrassed me. Her management of this bedtime interview was becoming positively matronly.

'What happened?' I asked lamely.

'I didn't think that Mummy was taking care of you seriously enough. I used that as an excuse to bring you some fruit from the dining-room table.'

'Really?' I laughed.

'Yes. I remember it very well. And you said from your bed: "I detest all fruit".'

'You must be making this up,' I said. 'I don't remember.'

'You see, I thought that's what you did when people were sick. You took them some grapes.'

'I really seem to have forgotten it.'

'"I detest all fruit." What an odd thing to say. I started to say it a lot myself afterwards. I drank all your Lucozade. And you held my hand.'

There was a touch of accusation in all this.

'Perhaps it was someone else,' I said.

'Oh no. You were you, all right. No mistaking. I don't suppose I really knew it properly at the time, but you were frightfully exciting.'

There was nowhere for this conversation to go. As she gave me a sudden tight squeeze against her stout quilted bosom, I had a sharp vision of Charlie Rivers sitting up in their bed, in pressed pyjamas done up at the neck, waiting for her to return, reading John Grisham beneath a flowered lampshade and finishing off his whisky. I remembered her twelve year-old knees, and I remembered her licking my nose, at an age when she could still be called 'Puggins', even if she didn't like it. I patted her back in a way that I hoped was sufficiently both tender and dismissive.

'What a long time ago that all was,' I said.

'Long ago and far away,' she replied, half-quoting the song, I thought. 'The script looks very childish, but think of it as a keepsake.'

She looked at me for a moment as though time had suddenly ceased to have any meaning at all. As though all possible futures were telescoped with all possible pasts. I felt peculiarly as though my face were an offered box of rather expensive chocolates.

'Well,' she said at last. 'I'll leave you in peace.'

Once the door had clicked shut behind her I could reflect more calmly on the actual passage of time. How strange, I thought, to have known someone fairly well on the very threshold of their sexual life and then to meet up with them quite by chance at the point when that sort of thing was all perhaps effectively over. I was making no assumptions about her and Charlie, of course, just as I had never wanted to speculate too closely about what she may have got up to with Ambrose Caiger or any of the delinquent posh thugs at her progressive school. It was just that the whole of her allowable romantic and child-bearing existence, that noble female purpose, had for me taken place off-stage. If 'off-stage' was the right way to put it. Probably it wasn't, since any real drama in our relationship was non-existent.

So I had been 'frightfully exciting', had I? This notion belonged to an entirely missing phase of my relationship with Margaret and had surely been developed in my absence by her feverish pre-adolescent fantasising. I found it hard to relate the confident quick-witted rebellious little girl I had once taught (the Margaret who frowned into hub-caps, in Maurice's memorable encapsulation) with the sentimental grandmother who had just padded out of the room. Hugging her seemed very little different from hugging my own grandmother, which cruel time had still allowed me for a time to do when I was in the RAF. Now very often the oldest person in a family gathering, I still felt passively young, likely to be on the receiving end of hugs and uncertain of the force of my opinions. Being hugged by the old Margaret therefore made me feel young and gauche again. I vowed to try to make some of this apologetically plain at breakfast, when I hoped that being less exhausted might encourage me to be more friendly and communicative. But I supposed that it would be impossible to admit that back in the Charlwood days I wouldn't have minded a bit hugging her all the time.

The room I was sleeping in was a sort of workroom, with a desk and files of committee papers of organisations that 'Mrs Rivers' obviously played a powerful part in. My eye strayed over these in a bemused acknowledgement of the busy life they represented. There were photographs here and there, mostly of young persons with the Dudley mouth and the Dudley jaw stopping in the middle of whatever they were doing to scowl at the camera. I looked for images of Maurice and found only one. Even that eluded me for a time, since he was wearing a shadowing broad-brimmed straw hat and a straggling greyish beard and was standing on the stump of a tree in a wood declaiming. Maurice in a beard! He looked like Walt Whitman. I supposed it dated from his Mapleleaf period, when he might have been in his late fifties. Looking at it more closely for clues, I saw that a young woman was just visible in the foreground, half-turning to the camera in amusement. Paula, of course, in an attitude half-tolerant, half-derisive, that was familiar to me. Paula being histrionically preached at. Paula ready with a sarcastic remark.

But I immediately realised that of course it couldn't have been Paula, even though it looked in so many ways exactly like the governing Paula that I remembered.

It was Margaret. It was a glimpse of Margaret in the careless ripeness of her 'off-stage' existence, not Puggins any more, and not yet, of course, Mrs Rivers, but a young woman in a wood in Vermont listening to her adored father say something ridiculous that was now lost for ever in the autumnal air. There was a line of vigorous animal attractiveness running from the turn of her head and neck, across an arm slightly raised as if to begin to gesture to the photographer, down the twisted spine, across the other arm that ended in a naked wrist hanging over a knee. She was beginning to look back at her invisible companion, to share with him her affection for this absurd orator, her madly bearded father. Perhaps the companion was the young Charlie, already critical of the oldest Beatnik there ever was. Or maybe an earlier admirer. No, certainly not Paula. Paula was probably already at that time elsewhere with her Stephen Stanger.

Before I went to sleep, I read Margaret's script for the Three Stooges film. Over that distance of time it seemed even odder to me that this crude vein of vaudeville comedy should have been so familiar to her. I thought of Maurice sneaking off with her to the Gloucester flea pit and buying her ice-creams. The script seemed to be telling me something that I hadn't fully thought through before.

The Three Stooges at the Dentist

Written and Directed by Margaret Clara Dudley Arne

Mo: ~~Annie~~ Ambrose
Larry: Pet
Curly: Margaret
Dentist: Johny
Nurse: Annie

Scene 1 In the Kitchen. Mo is writing his music on the kitchen table. Larry is tieing a piece of string to his tooth and looking for somewhere to tie the piece of string to.
Enter Curly who opens the refrijarator door and hits Larry in the eye.
Curly. Whats to eat? I'm hungry.
Larry. You just hit me in the eye stupid. He puts his two fingers into Curlys eyes.

167

Curly. Mmmm! Dont do that. Find me something to eat.

Larry. I made some very nice beans.

Curly. Beans beans, nothing but beans, I hate beans, mmm.

Closeup of a pan of beans.

Larry. Such a fadist. Beans are good for you.

Mo. Stop complaining. Im trying to be creative here. He hits Curly with the saucepan.

Curly. Mmmm!

Larry ties the string to the refrijarator door. Curly is inside the refrijarator looking for icecream.

Curly. Wheres the icecream?

Mo. Larry ate the icecream already.

Larry. How can I have eaten the icecream? I cant eat icecream ever again. Ive got toothache.

Larry hits Mo with the saucepan. Mo takes the saucepan back and hits Curly again. Curly takes the saucepan and hits ~~Mo~~ Larry.

Larry. Oh oh my tooth.

Mo. There isn't any icecream. Is there no peace in this house? Did Batehoven have to suffer this.

Mo slams shut the refrijarator door but the tooth does not come out and the string pulls Larry so that he hits Mo.

Closeup of Mo very angry. Steam comes out of his head.

Mo. I'm sick and tired of that tooth of yours, why don't you go to the dentist.

Curly. Then you can buy some icecream at the drug store.

Larry. A little sympathy wouldn't come amiss fellows. After all Ive done for you two.

Curly. Mo is writing a little sympathy, aren't you Mo?

Mo. I would be if I wasn't interrupted all the time. Im going to take you to the dentist and get some peace and quite if it's the last thing I do.

Larry. Im posatively terrified by the thought of the dentist.

Mo. Well do something about it then.

Curly. Never put off till tomorrow what you can do today.

Mo bangs Curlys head and Larrys head together.

Curly and Larry. Owww!!!

Scene 2 In the Dentists. There are screams from behind the closed door.

The Dentist comes out with a big pair of plyers.

Dentist. Get me a bigger pair of plyers will you.

The nurse opens the drawer and the Dentist takes out a big pair of plyers and a hammer and a saw. The Dentist goes back into his surjary.

Larry. Get me out of here.

Mo and Curly hold him down on his seat. Larry tries to get up and they tear out his hair in handfulls.

Larry. I can think of better things to do with my life than this. Why do I have to put up living with such layerbouts.

Mo. Take it easy.

Curly. Yes, take it easy.

Mo. Who told you to talk?

Mo holds Curlys nose and twists it round.

Curly. Ow!!!

Larry. I could just walk out if I wanted to. I could walk away.

Dentist. Next please.

Larry. You go instead of me.

Mo. Im not the one who has the toothache.

Larry. Its so bad its more like threethache or fourthache.

Mo. Well all be here when its over and well bring you some icecream.

Curly. Well be here for you.

Larry. Thanks fellows, that's real swell.

He goes into the dentist surjary. There are screams and shouts from the door. The Dentist has a big hand drill and drills into Larrys mouth.

Mo looks at Curly.

Mo. I cant stand pain. I don't deserve this.

Curly. Neither can I.

Mo. Lets get out of here.

Larry. But we said we would stay and look after him.

Mo. Whats the point? Ive got other fish to fry.

They tipto away.

Blood coming out under the door.

Mo is frying a pan of fish.

Curly. This is better than beans any day.

The End.

Despite the surprising shapeliness of the structure, it was indeed as Margaret had said, childish and short-winded. Her spelling made me realise that I had never asked her to write things down in her French lessons, and that I had been fooled by her resourceful argufying into thinking her more advanced than she was. But her evident view of Mo as a version of Maurice was a revelation, and I wondered if her connecting her domestic life with the anarchic violence of the stooges was an entirely subconscious affair. Was Maurice short-tempered within the bosom of his family? It was entirely possible. Had Paula's wisdom teeth really cast such a painful shadow into their lives? Who could say?

Tired as I was, it took me ages to get to sleep. I was running all sorts of scenes through my head: of the Americanized Maurice seducing his students; of Maurice in a dusty teaching room at the Royal Academy trying to keep a flame burning for Tchaikovsky and Rachmaninov and all the composers he really loved; and above all of Maurice as the vicious fringed Mo defending his work space. I imagined being back at Charlwood with the opportunity to work on the script and actually to make Margaret's film. I would have been the sunny centre of creativity and domestic harmony, and I would have cast the stooges as they were surely in an ideal world intended to be played, with the actual members of her immediate family.

20. Remembering

Charlie cheerfully drove us over to the nursing home ('Leave your own car here, old boy, and pick it up when we get back') in a 4 x 4 that smelled distinctly of dogs, though strangely enough I had seen none in the house. We travelled about thirty miles along the A47 to an overgrown village not far beyond Dereham. The nursing home had presumably once been the old manor house, rather grand in its gravel drive and leafy parking arrangements, though predictably business-like in its buzzer for admission, its leatherette and chintz reception area, and its white-coated staff and complex signing-in arrangements. As I followed Margaret and Charlie down the interlinked corridors, nervously preparing myself as for some unknown ordeal, I was warned of dementia, but at the same time was told in a fierce whisper that 'Daddy has read your books.' Which ones, I wondered? But that didn't seem to matter.

Nothing really seemed to matter in this carpeted world of beached bodies and missing minds. We spoke quietly and intermittently, as if in church, but since we had rehearsed only inanities in the car, largely in response to a topographical and agricultural running commentary from Charlie, that too didn't seem to matter very much. I certainly had nothing much to say. Somewhere in my fearful imagination was a scene from some Dickens novel, where the long-immured patriarch looks up brightly at the visit of his faithful daughter, for once wreathed in smiles of renewed hope at being exposed unexpectedly at last, after many delays, to the one character who is the key to the whole mysterious plot.

In life itself there are no satisfactory denouements. And of course, no plots. The little we know is, to be sure, forever at the mercy of perhaps uncomfortable enlightenment, but the deep puzzles of human relationships are gradually familiarised to us without the anxiety of having to solve them. In the end there is only one final question that stumps us. Seeing Maurice in his terminal frailty and stillness, I was instantly reminded of it. It's the old question of value and purpose. When the mind goes, where does it go? What happens to everything that it has patiently learned and empirically felt? What was it all for?

He was seated by the window, dressed, but imperfectly, as though not long out of bed. Since the latest image of him that I had seen had been bearded, I half expected him still to have one, but that of course had been a sort of backwoods or transcendentalist disguise belonging to his Francis Parkman period at Mapleleaf. Whatever strange hat or persona Maurice had adopted in his life, whether for an afternoon or a whole season, always had a dramatic point. The attitudes he enacted were part of his excited and ongoing argument with the world. The Maurice I found now, looking without interest at the chrysanthemums near his window and at the copper beeches at the end of the lawn, had nothing to say to the world, and nothing to say about it to anyone.

In whatever sense it was really Maurice, the fact impinged on me only hypothetically. I could have been brought to any such room, bleak and institutionalised as digs, and shown any simulacrum of an uncomfortably aged human being, creaking in his loose clothes, and I would have had similar thoughts. Which were about the pathos of outlasting the human envelope and the pity of physical persistence against the odds, and hardly at all about the individual sitting there. There was nothing I could see that was identifiably Maurice's, no book to act as a hook for conversation, no familiar picture, no evidence of his movement about the room. He was there in the room undeniably, but the characterless and

172

overheated space was essentially unoccupied. The same could be said of his body, in which the ropes of viridian veins curled up his bare arms like ivy throttling a silver birch and the tightness of the skin across the face in contrast with the hanging looseness of it below the chin gave his blank expression a vulture-like wattled querulousness quite unlike the face I remembered. The surface of his body was pale without relief, except for a liverish mottling and the bruising of the eye-sockets with their reddish liquid globes sunken in blotched and puckered skin. That thin and fragile skin itself seemed to be pinched and clustered round his features hastily as if the face was in the process of moulded assembly. There was nothing to animate the face, the arms, the dropped hands, the stiff parallel legs. Maurice was not there. But what there was, behind the generally lavender-pacified medicinal smell so characteristic of nursing homes, was a whiff of a more human smell, a proximity of plumbing. It made me remember Maurice's comic theory about roots, that loos were sacred temples of our contact with and worship of the earth. And it was a sad reminder that in our forgetting we ultimately lose all responsibility for our physical existence. I knew very well that the demented finally even forget how to eat and how to breathe.

I had rehearsed some remarks, naturally. I had been warned about what to expect, but I was still ready with cheerful ice-breakers. I somehow felt that the whole point of this expedition of Margaret's was that he would, after all, recognise me. I would be the very person to bring him alive, the unexpected key to his locked-in state. If not, what on earth was it for? But the witty or sentimental phrases were stillborn at my lips. They were quite useless. I might just as well have been suddenly transplanted to the Court of Imperial China three centuries ago.

Margaret had entered the room in a practical sort of way. She stroked his head and briefly held and squeezed his shoulders from behind, and then she had some flowers to change. Charlie had tactfully disappeared on the threshold. It was clearly up to me to take the lead that a visitor is expected to take. But no, I could hardly do it. I started to speak of Charlwood, of the passage of time, of how he must be proud of Margaret. That in itself was ridiculous. I knew nothing of his relationship with his once exasperating daughter over the last fifty years. How could you go on being 'proud' of your daughter in that sense when she was now an old woman fussing with a vase? I dried up, smiling foolishly. I wanted him to make one of his jokes.

He did turn slightly towards me at one point, and his lips moved uncertainly together to form something that might have been the beginning of a question, but his eyes flickered wildly away, and he gave only a sort of rudimentary sigh. It was as though his spirit had no strength to animate the body it was locked into. As though the weariness itself was burden enough. Did he remember me? How could he, now that I was no longer the person he had known? I looked nearly as old as he did, and absolutely strange to him. He would not remember me. And nothing that I remembered of him was truly helped or stirred by the terrible sight of this wraith in his ugly chair.

When Margaret had arranged the flowers, she sat down beside me and chattered away as she must have grown used to doing on all her visits. She spoke of many trivial things. She spoke at length about Charlie's geraniums. She spoke of me, and she spoke directly to me, as well as speaking to her father. I entered with some relief into this simplistic conversation with her, one designed entirely to inform and interest Maurice without the agonising requirement of a visible response. It seemed truly desperate and idiotic, but there wasn't much else to be done.

Before we left, I touched his hand and stroked it slightly. I would have liked to have kissed the top of his wispy head as a sort of blessing and farewell, but that seemed intrusive. I was unrecognised. And finally irrelevant.

I didn't blame Margaret for this unproductive visit. It was well-intended, and I felt honoured to have seen Maurice. He had been important in my life, and though I would now never know quite how I had figured in his, it felt significant somehow to have been allowed to appear before him again, a completion of something or other. On our drive back to Runcton St. Peter to pick up my car, I tried to say what I thought about his music as a way of reinstating him in my mind as his true self and not the shattered imposter we had just seen. I wanted her to give me instances of his later successes that I might have known nothing about, or of recent works that despite his illness were somehow ready for release. But she had nothing to say about any of that. Perhaps there was nothing. I dissolved into a sort of stunned politeness.

I thanked them both of course, and I wrote later to Margaret at some length to reinforce my thanks, and to tell her something of what I had felt. But what I really felt seemed too muddled with private matters to be communicated properly. It was then that I began to think that I might have to write it all down. If I did, would I get in touch with Margaret again to try to find out if she had any inkling of all the things that I didn't really know? I guessed not. She was both too close to them and too distant from them. I wasn't in the business of becoming Maurice's biographer. So this is really just a memoir. One brief view of it all, dredged up with appalling gaps. Memoirs can never be stories, can they? The author has barged in at least half-way through, and hardly ever sees things through to the end. What he sees is just a partial glimpse, and he has other fish to fry.

I have just put the CD of *Five Post-War Romantics* to play on my MacBook while I finish typing up these thoughts. His piano concerto is a strange sort of thing, really, heard in the era of Martland, Turnage or Adès. Its drama is so obviously staged or narrated—from the baleful opening roll of drums and the goblin waste land of the first movement, right through to the rhapsodic strings, glissandos and repetitions of aspiring chords at the close. I have now listened to it all once again, identified the Holstian marching rhythms and the Ireland-like clatter of the piano in the scherzo, its Rachmaninovian explorations in the moderato. It's a youthful and eclectic piece, but at its core is a serious question. I listened again to the opening of that final movement, with its searching, unlocatable melancholy and its little hopeful ascending chromaticisms, very much the heart-rending theme of the film. I listened to its sublimation much later in the massed strings nudged and worried by the interfering chords of the piano that seem either angry or puzzled that the orchestra is moving so determinedly to finality. 'Wait,' the soloist seems to say. 'Remember: there is so much to be done yet!' But the theme can't be repeated again with such conviction. The soloist is exhausted. You can see why it was so appropriate to that wretched film. Stewart Granger's understated decency, his double sacrifice, the conversion of his worldly happiness into something to be salvaged at last from his death ('I say, old girl, there's something I'd quite like you to do for me if you would. I don't suppose I'll get the chance now') all intended to symbolise, in their facile way, the transcendence of art. You can't help but be moved by the thought of Granger because you are moved by the music, which you can interpret as saying exactly that, but saying it better.

It has suddenly occurred to me that the student Maurice wrote the concerto for might have been Paula herself. Could she have been a student of his? Was that at all likely, in the middle of the war? Would she have been the right age? Well, it had to be someone, if Jack was right. And if it was Paula herself, after all, then she suddenly seems, in the light of that music, to have been a totally different person. But does that make her less or more of a mystery? Like Elgar's enigma?

She would have been the recipient and sacred guardian of that music, ventriloquising with the cosmetic voice of Patricia Roc all the false consolations that Muses and WAAF Ops Clerks are required to deliver to romantic heroes. And having to go on delivering them, what's more, throughout her life. 'Keep going, Doug, you've got to keep going. Don't give up. Don't ever give up. You'll get through!' Did she do that in private? Could she have possibly done it with conviction? No wonder Maurice became such a humourist.

But the pilot composer didn't get through. He died. And Stewart Granger died. And of course, Maurice died too, within the year. We all do.